𝕿he
GHASTLING

Book 12 Wales, UK "Cymru Am Byth"

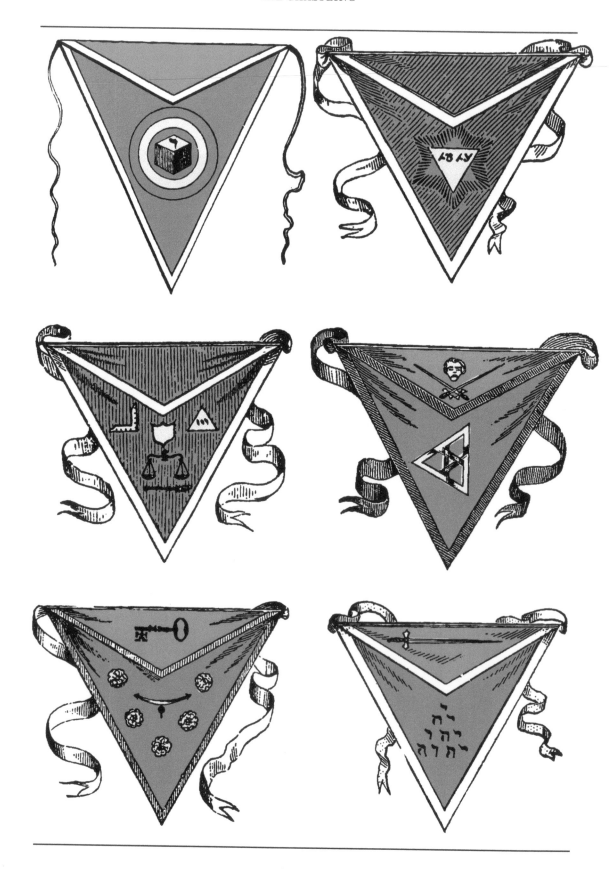

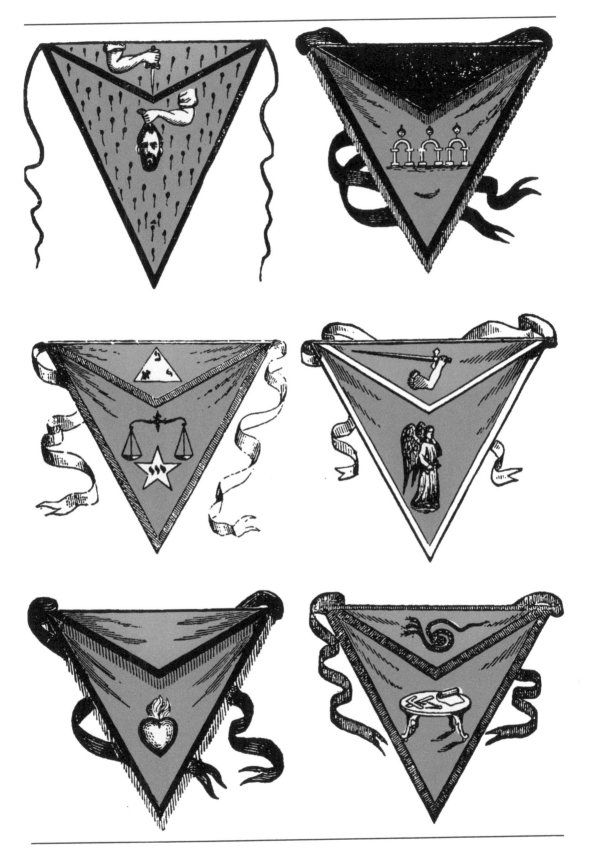

HORROR

2020, Book Twelve

The ghastling

Tales of Ghosts, the Macabre and the Oh-So-Strange

Editor
Rebecca Parfitt
Assistant Editor
Rhys Owain Williams
Art Director
Nathaniel Winter-Hébert

Special Thanks
Alex Stevens, J&C Parfitt
Contact
editor@theghastling.com
theghastling.com
facebook.com/theghastling

Published by **THE GHASTLING**

ISSN: 2514-815X   ISBN: 978-1-8381891-0-5
The Ghastling gratefully acknowledges the financial
support of the Books Council of Wales

ΘΕΟΝ ΣΕΒΟΤ-ΞΕΝΟΤΣ ΞΓΝΙΖΓ

Lesley Christie

Josh Keown

Victoria Day

Martha

Dawn Wilcox

Christine Pamela Williams

PATRONS OF THE HEADLESS HORSEMAN
to become a patron visit Patreon.com/TheGhastling

EDITORIAL

REBECCA PARFITT

artwork by Alex Stevens

Choosing the stories for this issue was harder than ever. We had three times the amount of submissions we normally get and the magazine could have been three times as big due to the great quality of the stories. I don't need to speculate why this could be, but I do think a few of you have had a little more time on your hands than usual!

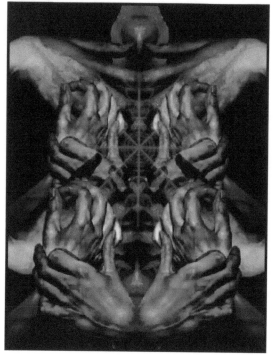

THE THEME of this one, **'Strange Signs // Ritual Protection Marks'**, was chosen by the wonderful Ghastling patrons – for whom I dedicate this issue. These generous folks have given me hope during a pretty bleak time and helped me to stay focussed on my goals for the future of the magazine.

While selecting stories for this issue, I considered the interpretation of protection: What are we trying to keep in? What are we trying to keep out?

It is human nature to want to protect what is yours and to mark your territory somehow. Humans have always loved to mark things: cave paintings, apotropaic markings, graffiti on walls, tattooing on skin. These could be interpreted as declarations of safety and of belonging; offerings of a belief and a connection to the spiritual. And an acknowledgement of the constant struggle between good and evil, too.

Everybody fears something (there is much to fear at present). But how many of us carry something tangible that we believe will protect us from it? Does acknowledging your fear make you feel stronger? Does that talisman around your neck make you feel safe? Or does it feel a little heavy sometimes?

I hail from Sussex, originally, and curiously the beaches there have very holey stones. It is believed if you place one of these stones – with a hole right the way through it – by your front door it'll ward off evil. So I have a few waiting to snare the Devil if he ever tries to get in. Ritual protection marks are used to protect our homes, where we feel safest, with a closed door to the horrors of the outside world. But sometimes I think, what if the evil is already inside, what is to be done then? I digress…

We are living in a time of strange signs and ritual protection marks where nothing at all is as it was. The chosen eight stories all stood out for their timing, their imaginative use of the theme – some interweaving the historic and folkloric together beautifully. But also because they gave us the chills, ultimately, it's the goose-bumps that I look for in a story. So I present the following tales for your delight:

Tom Johnstone's 'Creeping Forth Upon Their Hands' intricately weaves the events of the first English mass plantation in Ireland, at Munster, enforced under order of Queen Elizabeth I. This is a chilling contemporary ghost story masterfully told. In **K. M. Hazel's** story 'Devil In My Eye', a wanderer of the Black Country finds an abandoned farm to sleep in on a snowy night. Surely he should be comforted by the old tramp markings he sees there? This is a literary take on the 'slasher' and is a rare and delightful find for us. **Barry Charman's** 'Doom Warnings' is a great piece of dystopian horror for our time. A couple begin noticing 'May Contain Traces of Doom' signs on the packaging of their food. They avoid eating the food but soon they realise the rest of the people in their town are beginning to change … **Victoria Day's** tale 'Mr Price's Bed' is a brilliant

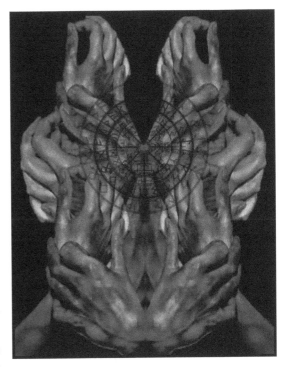

reimagining of the strange events surrounding Mr James Price's deathbed in 1658. What was it that possessed him and how could he have possibly predicted his own death? **Bess Lovejoy's** unsettling story 'The Nondescript' tells of a junior museum worker who finds an odd artefact in a drawer and shows it to each of the museum's experts – all of whom offer a different explanation. The last one she shows it to asks her to leave it with him. But what is it that she sees through the window? **Damien B. Raphael's** story 'Firstborn' is a wonderfully atmospheric tale about belief, witchcraft and the ritual protection marks and concoctions that are supposed to keep evil out … **Kristy Kerruish's** 'Night-treaders' is a creepy tale about a couple who renovate an old seventeenth-century lodge; a cautionary tale warning that some things found are better left where they are. Beware what blows in on the wind … In **Lucy Ashe's** story 'Where the Waters Meet', an anxious mother-to-be awaits the arrival of her twin babies. This is a sad and haunting story exploring the places we go to for comfort when we seek those we grieve for.

So settle in, light the candles and get the fire going – it's going to be a long winter. But don't worry, as long as you've got this issue with you, you'll be alright.

Thank you for reading – and don't forget to wash your hands before you cross the threshold…

Rebecca Parfitt
Editor

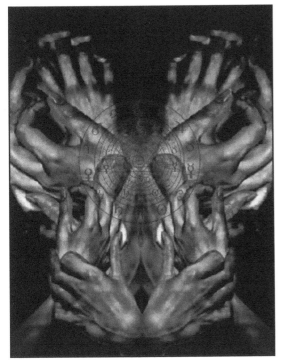

Nutrition Facts

Serving Size	250g
Servings Per Can	3

Amount Per Serving

Calories 450

	% Daily Value*
Total Fat 13g	20%
Saturated Fat 7g	37%
Trans Fat 0.3g	
Cholestrol 40mg	13%
Sodium 580mg	24%
Total Carbohydrate ...g	6%
Dietary Fiber 4g	16%
Sugars 7g	
Protein 2g	
Vitamin A	30%
Vitamin C	2%
Calcium	10%
Iron	2%

*Warning – may contain traces of doom.

DOOM WARNINGS

BY BARRY CHARMAN

Vince always read the small print. You never know what goes into the things you eat, he thought. You know there are colourings and preservatives, flavourings, of course. Even if you don't know what they are, you accept them.

But what were *Doom Warnings?*

VINCE stared hard at the tin of beans, the small print at the back of the can was quite clear.

Warning—may contain traces of doom.

What sort of doom? Worried, he read on, then started to examine other tins that were on the same shelf. He found similar warnings to the first.

Warning—may have been prepared in an area containing doom.

Warning—artificial preservatives/doom.

What *doom?* What the hell did it mean? He read and reread the cans until he convinced himself he wasn't going crazy.

There was doom in everything.

Vince bought some cans and took them home. He called up his girlfriend and told her, but she didn't believe him. Eventually he convinced her to come round, and watched nervously as she examined the cans.

Sally looked up at him, uneasy.

'Doom?' he asked.

She nodded. 'What does it mean?'

He breathed in relief. 'I don't know.'

She put the can down, then looked around at the cupboards in the kitchen. 'Have you checked anything else?'

Vince just shook his head. He hadn't dared. So they went through the cupboards, taking out jars and cans, turning them, examining them. There it was, time and time again, in the smallest, finest, print.

Doom warnings.

'Warning,' she read on the back of some washing up powder, 'check allergies to doom.'

She looked up at him, her hand shook slightly and the powder shook in the box. 'Whatever it is, it's in everything!'

They called the police, but no one took them seriously. It's just a word, they said, it was a prank, it didn't mean anything. So they went to the supermarket, but when they showed the manager, he just scowled and got angry. He thought someone was playing a trick, and went off to find somebody to fire.

Vince got home and looked up doom warnings on the internet, but he didn't get anywhere. He bought some cereal and studied the back, where he read that it *contains approximately 8 servings of doom.*

It took a week before a pattern emerged. The doom warnings were unique to their area. It was Sally who worked it out. 'These products aren't authentic,' she pointed out, showing him some of the shoddy labels on some of the cans. 'They're made locally; probably all come from the same factory.'

She wanted to go talk to someone, try and find the source, but Vince wasn't sure. Maybe they should just leave it, he considered; it wasn't like the products were *hurting* anyone.

Vince thought of his neighbour, he'd seen him only that morning, eating breakfast through his window. He was scoffing away, spoon after spoon. Vince had recognised the products as containing 'doom,' and he seemed healthy enough.

'We should report it.' Sally was getting nervous.

'Someone else will.' The more Vince thought about it, the more he wanted not to get involved.

Let it be someone else's problem.

They went to a restaurant that night, but neither was feeling hungry. 'I'm sure we're okay eating out,' Vince said, as he watched Sally push a fork around her plate.

She smiled hesitantly, but just as she was lifting the fork to her mouth, someone screamed.

Across the room, one of the other patrons had fallen face down into his soup. Opposite him, his wife put a hand to her mouth and looked as if she felt nauseous.

The rest fell like dominoes. Sally lowered her fork.

They each had something wrong with their skin. Some sort of lurid, grotesque, bruising was spreading all over them. Vince tried to help one person back into his seat, but he didn't like the weird way their flesh discoloured beneath his touch.

They left the rest to the staff, and Vince pulled Sally away. 'We can't help them,' he muttered. At the doorway, they glanced back at the chaos, then got out.

The next day there was a breakthrough. Sally got a tip from a friend who worked in the local environmental department, about a factory on the edge of town. 'It's new,' Sally explained, 'only set up a year ago. No details online, no history, nothing. It's passed inspections, but no one's happy about the place, the products are okay, but the people were

weird, detached.'

'Detached…' he echoed. Vince thought back to the restaurant, and how the only person who hadn't freaked out had been the manager. A curiously unmoved man, pale, uninvolved. New in town, it occurred to Vince, vaguely.

They exchanged a long look, and each knew what the other was thinking. They got into the car without a plan, just a need to know more.

Weirdly, all the people who worked at the factory seemed to have moved to the town when it opened. Vince gripped the wheel as he thought of all the new neighbours who had appeared lately.

'All these new people…' he muttered.

Sitting next to him, her thoughts running parallel, Sally nodded.

There was no security at the factory. It was like they weren't afraid of visitors. There was no staff, no sounds of activity, as if all the work had finished.

Climbing over an old wire fence, they found the first door they came to wasn't even locked. Once inside, they found the factory

floor abandoned. Just a vast open area, a dark neglected space that echoed their every step. Towards the walls were a series of giant, inert, machines. Each looked unlike anything they had ever seen before, and neither could imagine what function they performed.

'There's nothing here,' Vince said.

They were about to give up, when Sally found a small room and spotted some battered-looking lockers leaning in a corner. She went through them and pulled out some ragged overalls that had been left hanging inside. Going through the pockets, she found a scrunched-up scrap of note-paper and passed it to Vince.

I tried to warn people. I had to be subtle. Don't eat the food. They made us make it. We put things that were not of this world through the grinder. I don't know who they are or where they came from. DO NOT EAT.

Vince read the message, the last of the doom warnings, or the first, then handed it back to Sally. She read it, and then they stood in silence.

They drove back to town, each lost in their thoughts. They looked in at every restaurant, they parked outside the supermarkets, arguing over what to do, who to tell.

In the end Vince drove home, and knocked on his neighbour's door. He wanted to know if he *felt* any different, and if so *how*.

It was desperate, but it was all he had.

His neighbour was a middle-aged Scotsman. A town planner, or something like that, Vince had only really talked to him a couple of times. He seemed like a straightforward guy, kept his garbage neat and his lawn neater.

He opened the door and looked at Vince. His face was discoloured and bruised.

'Oh.' Vince didn't know what to say. 'Sorry, I just, uh, saw you through the window, you okay, man?'

'Me?' His neighbour smiled. It was an easy smile, relaxed. He didn't seem to be in any discomfort. 'I'm good.'

'Okay.' Vince nodded. His neighbour stared at him. It was a fairly penetrating gaze, and Vince had to look away. It was then he noticed his neighbour was using a pen in his right hand to write on his left arm.

The sleeve was rolled up, and Vince could just about make out the words as they were scrawled largely against the blemished skin.

'It's a lovely day,' his neighbour was saying, 'don't you think?'

'Hmm.' Vince was staring at the arm.

Warning – Changing. Locked in. Controlled. Not me. Run. Run. Run.

'I, uh, I gotta go–'

'Alan.'

Vince looked up. Alan was staring at him with a cocked head and a dim smile. A thin gobbet of black drool was leaking from the corner of his mouth.

The pen dropped out of his hand. It flexed, and one by one the fingers curled inward into a fist.

'Okay Alan, I'm glad you're okay.'

Alan smiled at him. Vince recognised his expression, it was the leisurely kind a cat knew when it was licking itself, and contemplating its next meal.

'Thanks, why don't–' Alan's face twitched, and a bloated black tongue briefly escaped his mouth before it was concealed back behind a row of sharp teeth.

'Well, seeya–' Vince was already moving.

'Why don't you come in, I was just gonna eat–'

He continued talking, but Vince was running to the car.

Sally was sitting inside, waiting. 'What's *happening?*'

He got in and stared ahead. 'We have to warn people,' he felt sick.

'How? What do we do?'

Vince glanced back, Alan was waving from his doorway, but he was twitching and jerking frantically, like an insect from another planet.

'Drive,' Vince said, 'and don't stop!'

Realising the town was doomed, they drove to the next. Vince rifled through the cans at the first supermarket they found, and while there were no warnings, he found more traces of the same fake labels, the same inauthentic products.

So they went to the next town and the next.

Eventually they knew what they had to do.

At each new place they stopped at, they brought pens, crouched down in the aisles, and wrote little warnings on all the dubious products they found. They spread these messages to anyone who might find them.

Whenever they were seen, they assumed the worst, and fled before there were any questions. At one point a checkout girl stared at them unblinkingly. As they backed away, she sniffed at the air as if her senses confused her.

In a chemist's, they watched a man read a message shortly after they'd left it. He frowned, then studied the product much closer. He dropped it into a basket after a laboured shrug. His skin was already blotchy. Was he doubling down, relying on the thing that made him ill to make him better? He was stuck in his rituals. Comforted by them.

Vince wanted to go after him, but what could he say? They only intervened when they saw children buying the tampered goods. Often, only the children listened.

Moving on, they bought samples and sent them off to newspapers, journalists, scientists, universities; encouraging them all to do tests. They did all that they could.

The story never broke. So they called their families, their friends, told them to listen, to spread the word as best they could. Half of them never even picked up.

Sticking to the cheapest, middle-of-nowhere motel rooms, they held each other and tried to think what more they could have done.

'It was all too quick,' Vince found himself saying. 'Too much too fast.'

Sally turned away, he watched her back shake as she sobbed into her pillow. The world as they knew it was slipping through their fingers, it was almost more than the mind could take.

Holding her, Vince understood it wasn't possible to save everyone else, but they could still save themselves, heed their own warnings.

Prepare for what was coming.

Understanding that this was an infiltration woven into an invasion, they started to watch out specifically for certain people. More and more they began to notice them. Lolling around on pavement like lizards; misshapen creatures who took their long slithering tongues out for a walk. It was then they realised any attempt to raise awareness was pointless.

They were no longer hiding.

Vince and Sally went to ground. They ran into a few others like them, and knew there was no choice but to band together and stay out of sight. They'd all picked up on whispers or started them as best they could. People were catching glimpses of something they knew was wrong, even if they didn't entirely understand what it was. Meeting Vince and Sally had probably been reassuring, for a moment.

After talk of fighting flared up, and the few that went to fight never came back, futility set

They ran into a few others like them, and knew there was no choice but to band together and stay out of sight. They'd all picked up on whispers or started them as best they could. People were catching glimpses of something they knew was wrong, even if they didn't entirely understand what it was.

in. They made a ramshackle settlement deep in the woods, a community for outsiders. They kept quiet and kept to themselves. Nothing came after them, so they felt safe, up to a point.

Every once in a while though, one of them went back to the cities, to try to see what was happening. Last time Vince had gone, he'd seen all the people changed, and not one human left. The things had shed their clothes, their illusions, all humanity had been discarded. They queued up at the markets and collected their food, waiting in some awful parody of what they'd once been. Vince had never wanted to go back, but after a while no one else wanted to do it either.

One last time, he thought.

He made his way back to the city, concealing himself whenever he could and watching the creatures from a distance. God knows what they would do if they caught him. There had been nightmares textured with this uncertainty. Vince had imagined being force fed, watched from giggling shadows by them as his flesh and soul warped to join their rank. He'd imagined toiling in one of their factories, or being slowly shoved piecemeal into a grinder...he watched them talk, watched them shop, he even saw two walking something that might have been a child.

Might it have been a human pet? He didn't look long.

Leaving with a rucksack of supplies that was only half full, he headed back to a car he'd hoped had room for any stragglers he might have found. There had been no people left, though. Just echoes.

Vince waited for night and used it to cloak him as he hurried away. Creeping towards the car, he kicked a discarded can, and picked it up before he left, curious. It wasn't until he got back to the camp and read the label, and then the small print, that he realised what he was seeing.

He hurried back to Sally, and thrust the can into her surprised hands. 'Read it!'

She read and re-read the small print, then looked up at him with a tense smile. 'You think...?'

'There's a new factory in town,' he said, 'there might be one of those things in there, but it looks like we built it.'

Warning—may contain traces of antidote.

CREEPING FORTH UPON THEIR HANDS

BY TOM JOHNSTONE

Sir **Edmund** *was an Undertaker when he first encountered the creatures.*

Not literally of course. 'Undertaker' was the curious name given to the settler-colonial administrators installed in the Munster province of Ireland during the reign of Queen Elizabeth I. The word may refer to the tasks these dignitaries had to 'undertake' in order to discipline the population. It is axiomatic that the imperatives of their role would have entailed the services of the other sort of undertaker.

ABOUT FOUR CENTURIES or so later, Dora Boyle takes the N7 from Dublin, merging into the M7 and M8 down to Cork, turning off onto the N72 to reach Mallow. As she drives south west, her PhD supervisor's mellifluous scorn rings in her ears.

'You mean to tell me you haven't even read *The View of the Present State of Ireland* yet?'

She has to admit she hasn't. Hardly the worst crime in history, but since her thesis is supposed to be on '*The Faerie Queene* and Elizabethan Polity in the Munster Plantation', she can see why he thought this was a bit of an oversight. Still, he didn't need to be so supercilious about it. She'll show him! That's why she's brought it with her to read as close as possible to Spenser's country pile, or what's left of it.

In any case, Professor Keenan had no reason to be smug, after what passed between them.

'You're twice my age,' she reminded him. 'And what would your wife think?'

'She needn't know,' was his reply. 'And as for the age gap, it never bothered Spenser...'

'This is the twenty-first century not the sixteenth,' she said, then left before he could start reciting *The Epithalamion* at her or something.

Maybe that was one of the reasons she's made this trip, mobile phone switched off. It might also be one of the reasons he's become a bit sniffy about her work lately. A bit of a break from the hothouse atmosphere of Trinity is just what she needs, even without his unwanted attention. She drives along the narrow country roads through flat, open countryside. She frequently has to slow down for horses. Sometimes a white woman shape huddles demurely among the leaves, a road-side shrine to the Blessed Virgin. The sky is leaden, and fat raindrops soon begin spattering the windscreen, but she doesn't mind. The rhythmic whine of the windscreen wipers is soothing, if a little plaintive. *Help us! Help us!* it seems to say.

A *wretched land, damp and boggy. After spending what felt like half a lifetime in Munster, that was Sir Edmund's abiding impression of the place. But for someone who had to work his passage through Merchant Taylors', a castle of one's own wasn't something to sniff at. It was just that trotting along the roads at night could be somewhat hazardous, even with an armed escort to protect you. One never knew when an ambush might burst from the quiet trees whispering in the wind. Cut them down. Raze them to the ground. Sow it with salt. That would flush out the damn bandits!*

Talking of damnation, the whole place was riddled with popery and idolatry too. They might say they venerated the Mother of Christ, but make no mistake, they meant the Magner Mater, *with all the licentiousness and degeneracy that implied. Might as well worship Circe! He wished he might call up Talos. Now there was a man who could flail some sense into them.*

There was some rumour going around that some of the Papist forces wore helmets and breast-plates that already bore the marks of a previous user. It was said an old woman dwelled in the bogs and wandered them in search of food and firewood. When she came upon a dead English soldier, she would remove his armour and sell it to her compatriots. Sir Edmund imagined her clad in blackened rags with an evilly-pointed nose. He thought of the old ballad about the two crows dining upon the new-slain knight.

> *'Ye'll sit on his white hause-bane,*
> *And I'll pike oot his bonny blue een;*
> *Wi ae lock o his gowden hair*
> *We'll theek oor nest when it grows bare!'*

He drove the Scotch gibberish out of his head. That was why it was essential to spread the English language as well as English ways. Ireland was a good example. No wonder the local population was so impudent and impious, when they still clung stubbornly to their native tongue. When you speak Irish, you think Irish.

As the darkness pressed in upon his convoy, like the mantles some of these bandits wore to hide their faces, he couldn't help remembering the final stanza of the border ballad:

> *'Mony a one for him makes mane,*
> *but none sall ken whar he has gane;*
> *Oer his white banes when they are bare,*
> *The wind sall blaw for evermair.'*

Dora stops off in Doneraile to pick up the keys to the airbnb from a gift shop on the high street. Smelling of scented candles, it's the only concession to tourists, and features tea-towels and other trinkets – some decorated with the ruins of Kilcolman Castle, others with something obscurer than this local landmark: hand-prints dotted around a patch of ashen ground.

'Good old-fashioned name,' remarks the shopkeeper as she signs for the keys.

'It's short for Eudora.'

'Grand,' the shopkeeper says drily.

'What's with the hand prints?'

'Oh that's just the hand-walkers' marks,' the woman says with a laugh, as if it's a silly question.

When Dora looks at her quizzically, her only reply is to point to another tea-towel design. On it, there's a reproduction of an old wood-cut, showing what appears to be a man doing a handstand, but with a face that's the right way up and positioned between legs that point skywards.

Sir Edmund woke with a start and lay there sweating in his vast bed. Just another nightmare in which the things were crawling towards him through the woods about the castle, moaning and gibbering. They were slow and weak with famine, but that did not matter. In dreams, one's own limbs were fashioned from lead. Besides, that wasn't the point. It was that these base creatures, dragging themselves like serpents through the mire, had human faces.

At times like these, he cursed his poetic sensibilities. He and Sidney had often discussed this problem. If only it were possible to instruct a gentleman in virtuous living without the need to wrap it up in some pretty story rendered in verse. Then it were possible for them to live untroubled by their imaginations. He wondered if these human beasts would haunt him thus if he were not a poet. But he was an Undertaker too. Perhaps it was part of his job to bury the past, or at least put it behind him.

He smiled as he turned to his sleeping wife in the bed beside him, her sweet face child-like

in slumber. Perhaps he should waken her and enjoy her favours, to put the terrors of the night from his mind. No, let her sleep. Such thoughts were put there by the Devil. He often wondered if the wily Earl of Cork had given him his daughter as a distraction, to tempt him into the ways of Popish licentiousness. But she was also a reminder, as the Queen's namesake, of his holy poetic purpose, a fit muse for him. Such was the duality of life.

Later, the steward took him on a tour of the grounds, showing him the strange markings in the dirt.

'Footprints, my lord,' the man said. 'Should I redouble the patrols?'

'Not footprints, sirrah,' Sir Edmund corrected him, pointing to the way the fingers splayed out, the thumb-prints too. But the steward stared at them stupidly, struggling to understand his meaning. Could the fool not see that they were the prints of hands? 'Your patrols will find nothing. Here's what you will do...'

I t's not hard to find the cottage. There aren't many houses near Kilcolman. She finds some provisions and a note left by the airbnb host, a Mrs Fitzgerald. It's full of the kinds of instructions and admonitions she'd expect, about the heating and the cooker and the recycling. But there's one rather unusual request:

'You may find small animal corpses outside in the yard. Please don't touch them or throw them away! They'll be gone before you know it, so don't pay them any mind. All the best and have a wonderful holiday, Irene Fitzgerald.'

What an extraordinary thing to ask! She certainly has no intention of touching any dead animals, apart from the bacon Mrs Fitzgerald has considerately left for her in the fridge along with some other fresh produce. Looking out of the window at the drizzle misting the panes and shrouding the land around the place, she won't be going outside today in any case. This seems like the perfect opportunity to sit down and read *The View of the Present State of Ireland* at last.

It's a good thing she's a captive audience here in the sticks. It isn't exactly a page-turner, just a tract about two blokes with Latin-sounding names discussing the cattle grazing customs of the Irish peasantry. Eudoxus argues they're practical and sensible, making maximum use of the land available. But *Ah!* says Irenaeus, it encourages rebellion, criminality and insubordination. If it weren't for your backward Irish grazing practices, he argues, we could starve the outlaws out.

Still, it's pretty dull stuff. In some ways she can see why Professor Keenan wanted her to read it. When all his other advances failed, perhaps he was hoping to bore her into submission. Inside the copy he lent her, probably as an excuse to gaze at her with his pathetic old puppy-dog eyes, he left a note inside the flyleaf, saying 'FAO Dora Britomart.' Hah! The token female knight in *The Faerie Queene*, who represents chastity. Funny how of all the virtues on offer, there's only one a woman can aspire to in Spenser's philosophy. She sees his game...

The professor's that is, the dirty old dog.

And she can see Spenser's too with *The View*.

Irenaeus moves onto the wearing of mantles, another filthy habit according to him. He's doing most of the talking by now. Poor old Eudoxus can hardly get a word in edgeways! It provides a disguise for your rebels, he says, a hiding place for weapons and can even act as a makeshift shelter for a miscreant on the run in a storm. It would have to be a pretty sturdy mantle, Dora thinks, looking out at the rain sweeping more persistently now past the window, to protect you against the Irish weather. But she sees a pattern emerging from this. It's what would now be called a Culture War, quite literally. For Spenser, Irish culture, whether it's the language, the clothes, the agrarian practices, even the bloody weather! – it's all a cloak for sedition. Basically, if you can't get them to bend the knee, you have to starve them into submission.

'Out of every corner of the woods and glens they came creeping forth upon their hands,' he writes of those starving after the Desmond Rebellion, 'for their legs would not bear them; they looked anatomies of death, they spoke like ghosts crying out of their graves; they did eat of the carrions, happy where they could find them, yea, and one another soon after, in so much as the very carcasses they spared not to scrape out of their graves.'

Spenser (or rather his author proxy Irenaeus) sounds as if he pities them, but his conclusion, calling the famine self-inflicted, makes it seem more like contempt.

The drumbeat of the rain that the howling wind now hurls at the panes isn't quite enough to cover the sound of something dragging itself along the ground outside the front door of the cottage. Probably an animal, but a large one that sounds like it's at death's door. Perhaps she should investigate, but it's dark now and horrible outside. She doesn't like the thought of any poor creature suffering, but she has no intention of going out there to look for it and nurse it back to health. She'll have a look in the morning.

A fter a few days of the things being nailed to posts outside the castle gates in the dog days, Elisabeth began to complain of the stench and the flies and the piteous sight of their grimacing rodent faces. He laughed at her beguiling soft-heartedness, but reminded himself this was part of God's plan to test him. He should not be deceived by her name echoing that of his Gloriana. She was her father's daughter after all. He was a knight errant and she the woman sent to tempt him with her wiles.

'But poor Peregrine...' she pleaded. 'The nurse tells me he was a-weeping to wake the dead with the night terrors all this last night, my lord. Methinks it must be these monsters you've mounted hereabouts, these gargoyles of flesh and blood as might be in the shambles!'

'Tush!' he scoffed, recalling his own evil dreams. 'I pray no son of mine will be a whey-faced milksop to cringe at shadows. Unless it be that he hath more of your woman's blood than he hath of my manly sap. I hope the latter be the case, for the beasts I have displayed outside are as nothing compared to what he'll doubtless see and smell in battle.'

They were after all just rats, when all were said and done, and dead rats to boot. But he wished the unseen creatures he kept hearing outside the walls would make haste and take what he'd left for them. The corpses were now so far gone, one could no longer see them for the glittering carapaces of the flies that swarmed upon *them! Perhaps that was the problem. The things turned up their noses at such rank carrion now, did they? So this was what happened when you appeased them. They demanded choicer fare!*

Then he saw his mistake, remembering those wretches he saw crawling from the woods and glens when the English forces humbled the treacherous Desmonds some fifteen years before. They lacked the strength to raise themselves from the dirt. He could hardly expect them to be able to reach rats atop posts.

The rain has cleared enough by morning for her to consider a trudge to the castle. But first she has to take a look outside to check for any mortally-wounded or dead animal that might account for the dragging noises she heard the previous night. Her search reveals nothing but some odd prints that remind her of the designs on the tea-towels and other trinkets she saw in the gift shop in Doneraile, in that they look more like hands than feet. Mrs Fitzgerald won't be happy with the damage to the grass, which the prints have churned to mud. Whatever made the prints has also flattened the grass with its weight, consistent with the sounds of the previous evening.

But what she sees next distracts her from fully digesting the implications of the markings. A half-eaten rat lies in the middle of the garden path, blocking her path. She could step over it, but she is so affronted by the sight and smell of the vile object that she grabs herself a shovel from the porch, scrapes it up and hurls it, gagging, into the yew hedge bordering the cottage garden. It's only afterwards that she remembers Mrs Fitzgerald's warning against doing this. She shrugs. She's damned if she's going to retrieve it and put it back where it was. It's probably some old Cork superstition, and she heard enough of those from her grandmother back in the day. She's not going to live by them now, when she's paying good money to stay here in some minimal degree of comfort.

The castle's a bit of a disappointment. Maybe it doesn't help that it's raining again by the time she gets there, soaking through her hiking boots and inadequate raincoat, so she can barely see what's left of it. She turns back before she can take a closer look after she nearly falls down one of the many holes that honeycomb the land around it. Stumbling around in the mist with them around is probably a bad idea, she concludes, especially given the big red sign saying basically 'Enter at your own risk!'

Glancing back she glimpses some large dark-coloured animal disappear down one of them, as if swallowed up by some vast, wet mouth. Something about it makes her shudder. She doesn't know why. Maybe it's the way it moves and the unexpectedness of its appearance; or it could be its resemblance, despite its crawling motion, to a man wearing some kind of voluminous hooded cloak, one that covers all its limbs, if it has any.

No, not the most appealing castle in Ireland, she thinks as she hurries back towards the car. But hardly surprising, since the rebels burnt it to the ground back in 1596, leading to Spenser's precipitate return to the more civilised world of Elizabethan London, where he died two years later.

'*Where is my babe, Edmund? Prithee tell me!*'

He laid his hands upon her shoulders, but her grief would not be assuaged.

'*Fie, Elisabeth. Weep not for him. He took his fate like a man at the end...*'

How much worse would her lamentations be if he told her the truth of what happened to the infant! For there were bite marks upon his dismembered remains. Aye! And the teeth were those of men. It was his belief that what took him was no mere rebel: not the mortal men that sacked Kilcolman, but some other fiend.

This confirmed his suspicions regarding the reasons for the creatures' refusal to dine on the rats he left, even when he took them down from the posts and left them on the ground where they might devour them with ease. They preferred finer meat – that of his issue and perhaps his descendants too.

When she gets back to the cottage, feeling the want of human contact rather keenly, Dora reanimates her phone.

There are half a dozen messages from Professor Keenan.

BEEP: 'Hi, Dora. Look, sorry about how we left things. I was out of order. Hope you got there okay and the traffic was... Just take care, okay? Bob.'

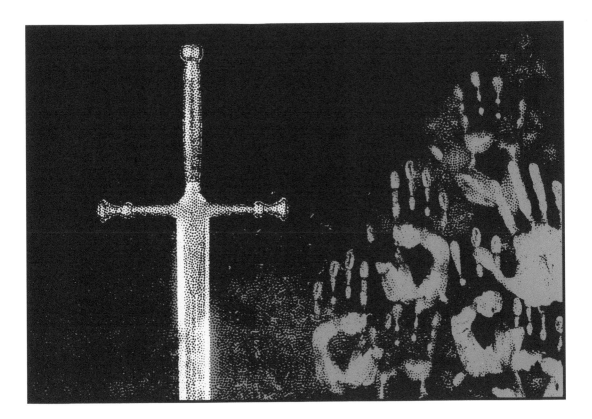

Well, nice he cares – not just after one thing – but 'Bob'! He always wanted to be on first name terms. She sees why now...

BEEP: 'Dora, I get that you're not my number one fan right now, but if you wouldn't mind letting me know you're okay, that'd be grand... Just grand.'

Sounds really worried. Or he could just be the controlling sort. That would raise red flags even if he weren't married and old enough to be her father!

BEEP: 'Listen, I did a bit of digging about the local legends. Well... You know how we were saying it was funny how you were called Boyle, Elizabeth Spenser's maiden name. Look, I don't want to alarm you or anything, but –'

She cuts him off, deleting the remaining messages. He's worse than her gran! She wouldn't be surprised if this were some ploy to frighten her into ringing him up so he could come riding down on his metaphorical white charger. Fortunately he doesn't know where she's staying.

Something drags itself up the path and hurls itself at the front door.

After the initial shock at the noise, she tells herself to think rationally. Even superstitions have their own infantile logic! The dead rat must be what they leave out for... whatever this is. It's just a matter of getting past it and retrieving it. Lovely!

She rushes out of the back door as the front door warps under further blows, then circles around to where she threw it. The yew's bristles scratch her bare arm as she rummages around feverishly, hearing the dragging again, nearer her now. It's almost dark, but she can just make out the grey fur in the gloaming. She reaches out and grasps it, feeling queasy at its soft, yielding limpness, but she'd rather touch that than the creature at her back whose rank breath she can smell. She throws the rat over her shoulder to draw it off, but it's like a cat that turns its nose up at what's offered and hunts wrens and sparrows instead. The pressure of its teeth on her neck and the rasp of the sacking covering the arms that enfold her in a bear-hug vice tells her carrion will not suffice this time, not when there's a Boyle to be had.

NIGHT-TREADERS

BY KRISTY KERRUISH

The feathers had once been smooth and iridescent, they had once melted the air in flight. Now they were crisp, dry and tortured by time. This feather must have been laid under the great oak beam when Brior Lodge was built in about 1600. The beam from the ceiling now lay across the floor, waiting to be fixed back into place. Jenny could still see the chisel marks where an axe had sliced against wood, darkened and patinated by the thousands of fires that must have been lit in the room over the centuries. It hadn't been easy to shift it, but it had shown signs of rot and a structural girder had been placed into the ceiling to support it.

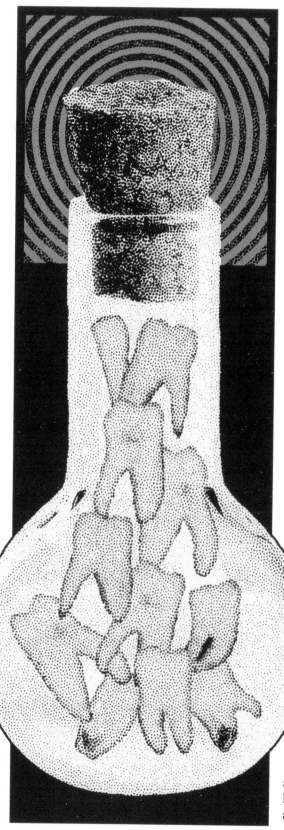

THE BIRD'S WING had been found under the beam. It was surprisingly well preserved. Jenny picked it up tentatively and took it to the window where the light was better. The walls of Brior Lodge were almost half a metre thick and the window recessed into them so that the ledge formed a seat. Jenny sat looking at the room, the great inglenook fireplace with bread ovens on either side and benches set into the stone. The rays of sunshine caught the dust in the air and burnished the stone flagged floor, smooth as skin. The original wooden partition screen, which had insulated the room from the cold air driven in from the main door, had had the layers of paint stripped away to reveal the original grain of the wood. Names had been carved into it, sometimes dates and pictures – the past was so close it was tangible. Brior Lodge needed extensive renovation, that was why Jenny and Trev had bought it. It came with its legends. When it was first built something terrible had happened, but it was too long ago to matter and since the day they had signed the contract Trev and Jenny hadn't had one moment of regret.

Trev had laid out the trophies on the table. 'Trophies' was Jenny's word for the collection of bones and bric-a-brac they had found: the bird's wing, several coins all discovered under one end of the broad beam. When they opened up the fireplace they had uncovered chicken bones and a small corked bottle full of teeth. Jenny placed the trophies in a shoe box. They were destined for the bin but Trev wanted to find out whether they were worth anything first.

Jenny pulled on her wellington boots. 'Trev! Are you ready?"

'For what?' Trev came through to the room, still dressed in his overalls.

'A visit to our tame archaeologist.'

'Kingsley?'

'It's only down the road so you don't need to change.'

Trev laughed. 'I wasn't going to. Got the key?'

'Yes.'

Kingsley's house was only three minutes down the hill, where a small ford glided across the road. The house was equally as old as Brior Lodge but, unlike Brior Lodge, it had been well maintained. The garden was tended and honeysuckle hung around the door.

Trev had laid out the trophies on the table. 'Trophies,' was Jenny's word for the collection of bones and bric-a-brac they had found: the bird's wing, several coins all discovered under one end of the broad beam. When they opened up the fireplace they had uncovered chicken bones and a small corked bottle full of teeth.

'Hey, you two. Great. Come on in,' Kingsley opened the door. He was a handsome man of about the same age as Jenny and Trev. His eyes lingered on Jenny's for a moment longer than they should have and she looked away self-consciously. They were only looks after all, and Trev never seemed to notice.

'We've got some finds,' Trev said holding out the shoe box, like a child might hold out a box of snails to a doting uncle.

'Come in and I'll put the kettle on.'

Kingsley walked ahead of them down the corridor, lithe as a panther, stooping his head under a low beam. He lived alone, but Jenny had never been too sure...she'd seen a woman. At first she had thought it was the cleaner, the place was always immaculate. Later, she had found out it was the wife of someone in the village. There was a whiff of village scandal in the air.

'Your kitchen's perfect,' Jenny said, looking about her. 'I love your Aga. We've got a long way to go before we get such a homely feel to our place.'

Kingsley gave her an open smile as he filled the kettle and set in on the Aga. 'So what's in the box?'

Jenny wrinkled her nose. 'Things we've found. Coins, a bird's wing and some chicken bones. A corked bottle as well. We just wondered if you'd be able to shed any light on them. You know about these kinds of things.'

Kingsley knew a lot about local history and about Brior Lodge too. It wasn't surprising, he was an archaeologist and historian by profession.

Kingsley opened the box enthusiastically and gave a grimace. 'This is a witch's bottle. They're gate-keepers. They're not worth anything now.' Kingsley put the lid on the box and pushed it across the table. 'You see, you've brought them out of the house now so they're useless. I mean, their power's gone, blown away.'

'What's blown away.'

Kingsley gestured for them to sit down at the kitchen table and poured the tea. 'Truth is, it's all superstition. In the 1600s people believed in charms and spells to keep away evil, all that's dark. All the shadows that no one understood but knew to fear.'

'Like what?'

Kingsley shrugged. 'Want a biscuit?'

'No thanks.'

Kingsley took a chair and looked at his cup of tea for a moment chewing on a biscuit. 'Let me put it this way, the people who lived in Brior

Lodge were afraid. They feared failed harvests and blighted crops. They feared the springs might dry up. Most of all they feared the *Night-treaders*.'

'Local superstitions?'

'Yes. The people who lived in Brior Lodge built these birds' wings and bones into the fabric of the house to protect themselves. These bits and bobs were guardians of the windows, the chimney, the doors – so that the *Night-treaders* couldn't blow in with sugar stealers or autumnal leaves.' Kinglsey looked at the window.

'What are sugar stealers?'

'It's the local name for dandelion seeds, they blow like thistle down. You see, under your roof these things still had a purpose. Now they're useless. You can't put them back.'

'We don't need to,' Jenny laughed. 'It's just foolish superstition. You said so.'

'Did I?' Kingsley hesitated. 'Thing is, when you get back you'll need to shut the windows at night. Even if it's warm, shut them. Bolt the front and back doors and put salt in the fireplaces, just in case'

'Salt?' Jenny gave a laugh.

'It's just superstitious nonsense, but all the same...'

They were back home at Brior Lodge within the half hour. Trev bounded up the stairs.

'Did you douse the fire?' Jenny said, stepping into the main room. 'The embers have rekindled. We should've left the guard up. It's cold in here.' The fire spat, Jenny saw the sparks skitter across the floor. She could hear Trev walking upstairs. 'Hey Trev!' Jenny stopped and, leaning her shoulder against the wall, listened to his footsteps steps moving against the shifting floorboards. 'Fancy a glass of wine? There's a bottle in the fridge.'

'Sounds good. Just closing the windows.'

'Oh, come on. You didn't believe all that did you?'

Trev's footsteps upstairs stopped suddenly. Jenny peered up, she couldn't see clearly but there was a shadow thrown against the wall where there hadn't been one before.

'Trev, come here!' she shouted. 'Trev?'

A cobweb shifted in the draft, there were sugar stealers snagged on its threads. Jenny frowned, it wasn't the season for sugar stealers. Cold air rushed in, taking up the dead leaves in an eddy. Jenny's brow furrowed into a frown as she

'Yes. The people who lived in Brior Lodge built these birds' wings and bones into the fabric of the house to protect themselves. These bits and bobs were guardians of the windows, the chimney, the doors – so that the *Night-treaders* couldn't blow in with sugar stealers or autumnal leaves.'

locked the front door. The hallway seemed to have gathered shadows. She listened to the silence, there was the sound of someone outside, the gravel giving slightly as their weight shifted.

'Trev. Get down here.'

The sound stopped and something struck the door. Jenny backed away as the blow came again.

'It's only me,' Kingsley's voice made Jenny gasp.

Jenny gave an embarrassed laugh as she opened the door. 'You scared the life out of me.'

'I brought you a book. Thought it might interest you.' Kingsley handed the book to her and smiled, catching her eye and holding her gaze. 'It's about the Night-treaders.' He watched her locking the door behind him.

'I'm not really interested but thanks,' she said, taking the book from Kingsley.

'No chicken bones and bird's wings for you Jenny. But we still have our guardians don't we; electrical alarms, smoke alarms, keys – that kind of thing. We rationalise our fear, explain it away.'

'Just being careful,' Jenny smiled. 'I'm not superstitious. We were just about to have a glass of wine. Join us?'

The wind blew some leaves in under the door. Another draft stirred them.

'See, my name's here,' Kingsley ran his fingers across the wooden panels.

'Kingsley. I never noticed,' Jenny laughed. She paused. 'There's a date?'

'I carved it myself, the last time I was here.'

Kingsley had never been in the house before, he had always declined their invitation. He had always stayed at the doorway when he'd called. He had never crossed the threshold until that evening.

'The date is 1600,' Jenny frowned. 'It says something else. *Blown in with the sugar stealers,*' she muttered.

What were sugar stealers? Something that blew in the air with ease, light, airy and beautiful. Something you didn't fear, carried on a gust of air.

Jenny looked at the title of the book Kingsley had given her. *'The Night-treaders: The Legend of the Shape Shifters.'*

Kingsley smiled. 'You've let me in.'

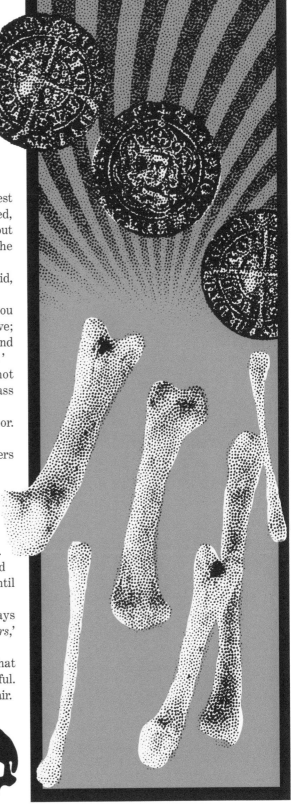

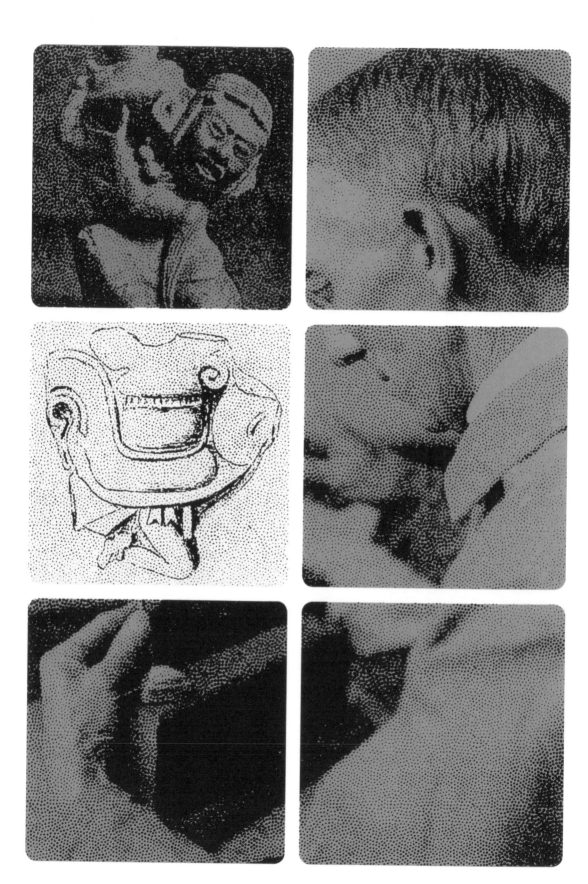

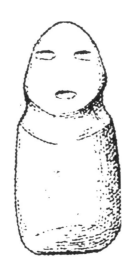

THE NONDESCRIPT

BY BESS LOVEJOY

I found it in the bottom drawer.

The sun had just set, and my head was swimming
with that late afternoon fatigue that comes mostly
from monotony. My shoulders had ossified into an
unnatural hunch over my work bench, and a growing
nugget of despair was lodged deep into my stomach.
All day long, I'd had just one task: removing artifacts
from dozens of sliding steel drawers, checking their
labels against typewritten cards in an ancient plastic
binder, and returning the artifacts to the drawers.
Items logged: 247. Items to go: 368.

FIFTEEN MINUTES before quitting time, I pulled a bottom drawer open and heard something clattering around. I squatted down, reaching my arm deep into the drawer, and felt my fingers brush against something rough and serrated, like a pine come. But as I fished the thing out into the light, I could see that some parts were smooth or only faintly nubby. As I turned it over in my hands, I noticed that it spiraled upward like a shell, only without the graceful regularity of a shell. The bottom bulged out unhandsomely. I suddenly felt a great affection for it, even though I had no idea what it was.

There was no box. There was no label.

'Bob,' I said. 'What is this?'

Bob, our director, was reinforcing the joints on one of our pre-war wooden cabinets. It was a task that wasn't supposed to be his, but that he liked to do rather than let other people try and mess it up, as he believed they inevitably would. I held out the thing to him, sweat beading on my palms beneath it.

'Where'd you find that?' he asked, wiping his screwdriver on a rag. His eyes were a pale blue-grey, the wrinkles next to them tiny riverbeds that branched into streams near the sea of his white hair.

'Bottom row of the Central American specimens to be deaccessioned,' I replied.

Bob wasn't paying a great deal of attention. He'd turned away and was sliding his tools, one by one, into a battered tin toolbox that was probably older than I was.

'Will you just look at it, Bob?' I asked.

He turned his gaze from the toolbox and toward my hands. I watched him narrow and then widen his eyes a couple times, as if in disbelief.

'I think I'm getting a headache,' he said finally. 'Or that thing makes my eyes hurt, it's so ugly. Look, it's almost 5:30. Why don't you bring it to Jon tomorrow?'

Jon was our Central American expert, and usually in a better mood than Bob, so I agreed. I'd only been at the museum a few months, and my contract lasted just a few weeks more, but until then whatever was in the sliding drawers was my temporary kingdom. Everything inside them was to be deaccessioned—sold off or otherwise disposed of. It was a small museum, after all, without the space or the resources to care for everything that had been collecting in its storerooms for the better part of a century. This part of Pennsylvania had once been wealthy, home to a number of 19th-century collectors, though mostly those not esteemed or monied enough to contribute to the big museums of the East. Still, they were capable of building up sizable stores, some of which made it to our display cabinets and, increasingly, to our basement.

My job was to make sure the cabinets of things no one wanted lined up with the binder of things no one wanted, so I could write up the deaccessioning report. If this thing wasn't listed in the binder—and without a label, it was hard to tell—it was a reject among rejects. That imbued it with a weird value in my eyes, like that thing they say about the enemy of your enemy. The reject of the rejects must be important, I decided, as I nestled the mysterious thing into some cotton padding in a cardboard box for safekeeping. I slid the box back into the bottom drawer, and pushed it closed, the clang of the metal reverberating in the room.

I brought the thing to Jon's office the next day. He'd recently come back from a trip to Costa Rica, and had a browned complexion I knew would fade quickly in the Pennsylvania

winter.

I'd caught him finishing lunch—almost always the same thing, a tuna sandwich from Subway—and as I walked into his office he wiped his mouth on one of the piles of coarse napkins they always gave him.

'Jon,' I said, uncovering the box, 'What do you think this is?'

He peered at it. 'Where'd you find that?'

'In the bottom drawer of that cabinet of Central American artifacts we're deaccessioning. But there's no label for it.'

I hoped there was no trace of tuna left on Jon's hands as he picked up the object. He held it up to the weak sunlight filtering through the windows, and I noticed a strange, dark-red gleam in one of its bumpier corners. Somehow, the color made my eyes sting.

'My guess,' he said, 'is that this was on the business end of a spear. See that red tint? That's the crushed residue of the *Diamphimea inperspicuus* beetle, which is poisonous. It's a type of biological warfare, if you will. But it's usually found in Africa, not Central America.'

I stared at the thing again. Its shape now seemed slightly malevolent, but something didn't add up. 'But it's not...pointed, like a spear would be, wouldn't it?'

'I think it's been degraded over time, which is why it has that weird lumpy appearance,' Jon

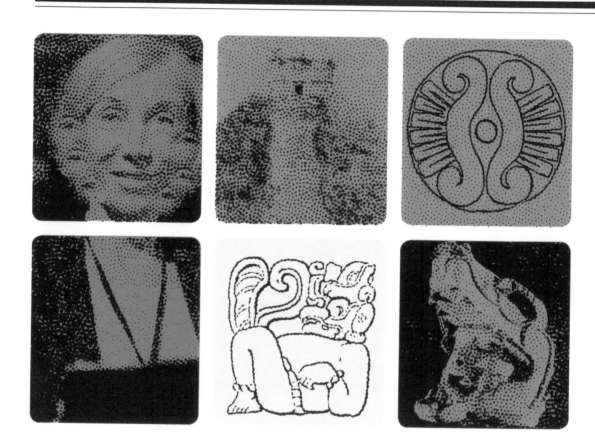

responded. 'There was probably something more threatening attached to it at one point, but it's gone now. Why don't you ask Coleen?'

'**N**o, no, no,' Coleen said moments after I entered her office. 'It's definitely not a spear.'

Coleen was our weapons expert. She had one of the better offices in the building, with dark oak paneling on the walls and a handsome suit of armor in one corner. Her necklace glittered against her gray sweater, which almost perfectly matched the silver of her hair.

'You see this mass at the top, how it's all round? How would you have stuck anything in there? There's no hole! Jon is off his rocker, as usual,' she laughed.

'So what do you think it is?' I asked, laughing a little nervously in response. 'I just want to, you know, have the record as clear as possible for the deaccessioning report.'

'Hmm,' she said, leaning back in her chair, creases appearing on her otherwise-immaculate forehead. 'I think it's probably purely ceremonial. Actually, I'll tell you what it reminds me of, but I should warn you it isn't very pleasant.'

'I don't mind,' I said. I could feel my eyes widening a little as I said it, and I hated myself for it.

'There have been reports, not entirely

reliable, that certain indigenous peoples have a coming-of-age ceremony when the women first menstruate. They mix some of the menstrual blood with whale blubber or other fat, rub it into long pieces of cord or string, and then wrap it around various rocks and shells. The women carry it with them until the birth of their first child, when they usually bury it somewhere underneath the floor of the menstrual hut. It's a charged object: very powerful, but very unclean.'

We both looked at the artifact in its box, which she had set down onto a pile of papers on her desk. I could imagine that it was made of rocks and shells and twine and blood, but there was something else there too, something softer, that seemed to be woven throughout its nooks and crannies. It was like a very fine lace or netting, but almost transparent; it seemed vegetal, as if shining a light onto it might reveal a pattern like the fractals of kale, or maybe the long fibers of celery. Or maybe the material did have something to do with an insect: parts of it seemed to have well-defined segments of butterfly wings.

'I'd take it over to the Earth Science department,' Coleen said. 'It's at least partly a rock, or once was.'

Paul was the only one of the geologists I'd been able to get to speak to me. They were a gruff lot, prone to muttering, and I always felt distinctly young and female in their presence. But Paul had kind eyes and bright white teeth that shone every time he cracked a grin, which was often.

'Ooh, what'd you bring me?' he asked when I entered his office. His low green desk was strewn with papers. Shelves lined the walls on either side, holding specimens in various states of classification and restoration—rocks the color of seaweed and electric light and bruised bananas and the first part of dusk. Unlike Coleen, who always seemed to be on show, and Jon, who kept his office spare, Paul had created a space that hummed with contentment.

I took out the cardboard box with the thing in it.

'Whoah!' Paul said. I wasn't sure if he was just humoring me, but I appreciated the enthusiasm.

'This is indeed weird,' he said as he took the box from me and lifted the lid slightly. 'Did you know it's seeping?'

He lifted the thing up. The cotton batting I'd arranged below it was damp, soaked in strange colors. The mess reminded me of the cotton balls I used each night, after I'd soaked them in makeup remover and wiped them across my face: a little brown, a little orange, and several streaks of red all mixed together.

I raised my eyebrows and shook my head. It hadn't been wet the last time I looked.

'Don't be alarmed,' he said. 'It's not all that unusual. There are some rocks that have networks of channels within them that can carry fluid. Occasionally you hear about it when someone discovers a Virgin Mary statue that's supposedly been crying.'

He picked the thing up and turned it around. 'Tell you what,' he said. 'I can't see crap in here. One of the light bulbs just burned out. But why don't we scan it with the electron microscope and see what happens?'

He took the thing into a little wing of the office I hadn't noticed before. There wasn't room for much more than Paul and the machine in the alcove, and I could only stare at the back of his corduroy jacket as he bent over the large hulk of gray plastic and metal.

'This is some weeeeiird shit,' Paul said.' There are holes in here, fractures that don't make sense. It's definitely not just one rock. However this was created, it wasn't a normal geological process.' He paused for a moment, and made a clicking sound with his mouth.

'I'll tell you what I think,' he said, and paused for dramatic effect. 'I think it's teeth.'

'Teeth?!' I exclaimed.

'Yeah. I mean, not entirely. But I think maybe some Bronze Age dentist—I have a feeling this thing is very old—had a little cache of molars he was carrying around. Maybe it was some kind of charm to ward off toothaches. Maybe it was a token of his handiwork. Who knows. But you know what I'd do? I'd show it to Henry.'

Henry was our odd-stuff specialist. He was hired as an expert in conchology—the study of shells—but since we were a small museum, he ended up having to consult on a lot of things that didn't quite fit the categories. One time, when someone tried to donate a collection of historic material from a nearby brickworks, they ended up with Henry, who had to patiently explain that we just didn't have the facilities to store eight tons of very notable clay.

By the time I brought the thing to Henry— I'd had to wait a week or so while he was out sick—the cotton batting beneath it was soaked all the way through. It looked redder, almost like a wound, although I told myself the color was probably just iron deposits. I couldn't figure out how it had stayed dry at the bottom of the deaccessioning cabinet for the past however many years and only now become so damp. Paul had said it was 'seeping,' but I was starting to wonder if it was actually … bleeding.

'Teeth?!' Henry said when I started to explain the story to him. 'He thought it was teeth?! That's the thing with these geology guys—they love to come up with the most exotic explanations. I think they have a complex because they study rocks all day and they know everyone thinks they're boring.'

I laughed. I set my bag down on his desk and pulled out the cardboard box, then lifted off the lid. Inside, the thing glimmered wetly. As Henry bent over it, we both heard a distinct, but very faint, shriek.

'What was that?' I asked.

'What was what?' Henry said.

'You didn't hear that?'

'I heard a little something, but I thought it was the pipes. They make strange noises all the time in this room.'

He bent over it again. This time the noise came louder—a tiny but crystal-clear wail. Henry grabbed the lid and stuffed it on top of the box, hastily enough that a bit of the soaked batting still stuck out the side.

'I think you should leave this with me,' he said, suddenly stern. I could see furrows in his forehead I'd never noticed before.

I did as I was told. But as I went out and closed the door behind me, I felt a pang of regret. I'd grown a little attached to the thing, whatever it was. After spending months with the museum's experts, normally so sure of themselves, I felt a tiny bit of pride in surprising them. At least, the ones who would admit to being surprised.

I left Henry's office with a frown. As soon as I turned the first corner in the hallway, I ran into Bob.

'What's going on?' he asked, looking mildly concerned. It was a rare show of interest in my well-being.

'Nothing much,' I lied.

We chit-chatted for a few minutes and then

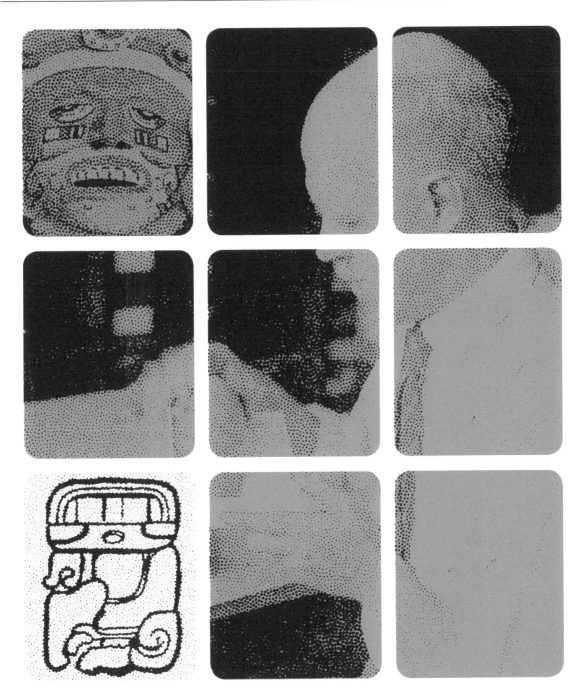

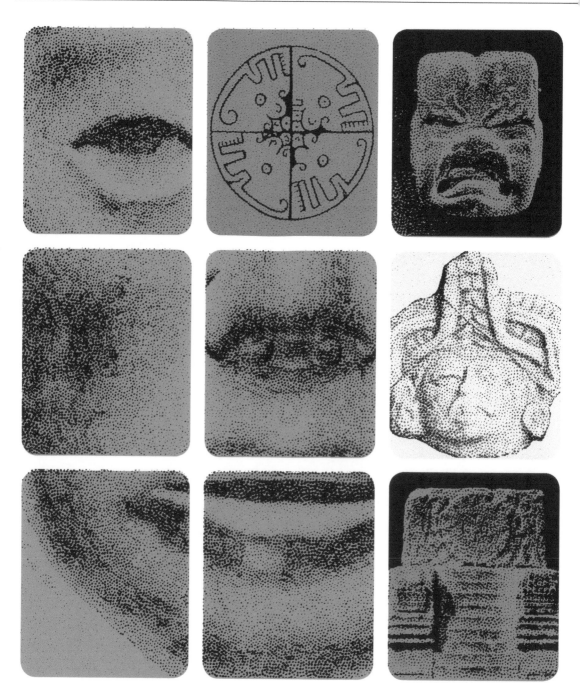

he asked, lowering his voice just slightly, 'Hey, that thing, that thing that you found in the de-accessioning cabinet … did you ever find the story behind it?'

'No,' I sighed. 'Jon said it was part of a spear. Coleen said it was some sort of ceremonial womanhood charm, or something. Paul said it was teeth? And Henry …' I trailed off. 'Henry's running some tests, I think.'

'Well, maybe you're better off not knowing,' Bob said. 'It could open up a whole can of worms. Whose department is it? How did it get in that cabinet? Where did it come from, and'—he widened his eyes theatrically—'what does it want?'

I laughed. 'Thanks, Bob,' I said. 'It was just a little mystery I was trying to solve. But it seems I failed, at least for now.'

'Hey, kiddo,' he said, raising his hand and waving it in the air a little, as if trying to waft away a bad smell. 'Failure's just the flipside of success. And half the time, success just gives you bigger problems to solve. Besides—there is another possibility.'

'What's that?'

'It's not your fault if that thing belongs to a category that hasn't been invented yet.'

At that, he turned and walked down the hall, humming ever so quietly to himself.

I worked late that night, trying to vacuum out a few decades of dust from one of the Peruvian cabinets. The room I was in was on one of the building's top floors, and as I aimed the vacuum hose into the grooves on the sides of the cabinets, I saw a light out in the yard.

It was Henry.

I felt a little yelp escape from my mouth when I noticed the lantern on the grass next to him, and a little backpack next to it. I watched him

unzip the backpack's front pocket and take out the box—my box. For a second, he appeared to be murmuring to it, stroking the top of it, almost petting it. Then he set the thing on the grass and picked up a shovel I hadn't noticed before.

The banging was loud enough that I could hear it on my floor. He smashed, smashed, smashed it to bits, with metallic clangs as the shovel connected to the object's sharper corners. I thought I could hear a little pitiful whine, but after a moment I realised it was only my own voice rising inside my ears.

And then, Henry started digging a hole.

By the end of April I had almost finished matching the contents of the cabinet with the contents of the binder, when, on the last page, I found a category that I swear hadn't been there when I started. The typewritten header said 'Miscellaneous.' There was only one item listed beneath that, but someone had smeared white-out across it. I thought for a second that I could see the ghostly outlines of the letters beneath, like twigs caught just under the surface of an icy pond, but they evaded my attempts to read them.

There was only one thing legible: in ballpoint pen, right next to the white-out, someone had written just one word in all caps: DESTROYED.

MR PRICE'S BED

BY VICTORIA DAY

MANUSCRIPT *of part of a diary [1658] sent to St Fagan's Museum, Wales, in May 2020 by Mr D Price. This is part of some family papers passed recently to Mr Price that he thinks may relate to the oak bed at the museum.*

27TH MARCH 1658

MY BROTHER James has returned from America. He sent no letter or warning, though he has been in Plymouth after his ship docked there for over four months. This is only to be expected, for he has never showed nor cared for any creature than himself in his life. I can only thank God that Mother died when he was away, and that Father died before he went. I believe that he broke both their hearts. The child he got upon Carys Rees is now seven years old, but I am glad that he knows only Gethin Thomas as his father. God knows how he would have grown up if he had my brother as an example. I hope that James does not mean to cause trouble.

He strode into my shop and, banging a fist on my counter, cried 'Do you not know me, Brother?'

I nearly staggered back at this apparition. I knew him instantly – that brash, clanging voice. If he was expecting a warm welcome, he was to be sorely disappointed.

I grunted at him and said, 'Well, you are back then?'

He stared at me then said, 'Don't fear dear brother. I want nothing from you for I have made my fortune in America. I have taken the house near the Church on a year's lease and have brought much of my own goods and furniture with me. All bought in Portsmouth and finer than any you may find in this hole!'

That did anger me, and I said rather hotly 'Hole is it? Well, if it is not good enough for a gentleman like you, then go away again. For there will none be here who will welcome you!'

At that he only laughed. Then he stopped and looked seriously at me. 'I have my reasons for coming home to my birthplace, David.' Then he left, banging my door so violently that some paint was knocked off.

This evening, I told Mary my news. She was worried as she knew of James' reputation from village gossip. She had never met him, thank God, and I was determined that I would keep him away from my family. She was worried that perhaps he wanted to see his son. I calmed her fears as I knew he would get nowhere with Gethin and Carys standing guard. No, there was something more behind this return. If he was the rich man now, why return here? I think that, despite his bluster, he is a frightened man.

30TH MARCH 1658

I HAVE SEEN little of James. It seems he keeps indoors in his own house and does not even venture to the inn. He knows the sort of welcome he would get there, but even so I am uneasy at this unusual behaviour of his. He was, before his flight to America, very much the man for company and merry making. His housekeeper is a local woman, Mrs Bowen, who is a hard-faced and close-mouthed woman. James has chosen well. Gossip has found me out in my shop whether I want it or not. The neighbours have told a good deal of information. From dusk he wanders in the graveyard until first light. I doubted this very much at first, but I heard it from two good sources. He was seen by our physician Dr Powell on his way back from a patient at about one o'clock in the morning. I asked him about it and he told me that James was walking ceaselessly to and fro and muttering something in a prayer-like way, although to him it did not sound like prayer. Dr Powell said he had heard from folk coming in from the fields of seeing him several times there. One fellow, Samuel Howells, went into the yard to ask him if he was well. He was almost knocked over as James lashed out at him in a blind fury. Then, seeing that it was Sam, he mumbled an apology and continued on around the yard, mumbling words that were neither Welsh nor English. I am not sure what to think.

19TH APRIL 1658

THIS MORNING our maid Jenny came bowling in at breakfast with the news that her sister who works at the Inn had been woken at dawn by a hammering and shrieking at the door. The landlord, Mr Richards, found the normally stone-like Mrs Bowen in a faint. She was brought in and looked, apparently, like 'a dead corpse, all white and black round her eyes'. She had been shaken and then beaten about by James in a fit of deadly anger and then thrown down the stairs and out of the house. Once she had composed herself, the tale was told. She had been awakened early by a strange sort of low groaning from her master's bed chamber. She

> Gossip has found me out in my shop whether I want it or not. The neighbours have told a good deal of information. From dusk he wanders in the graveyard until first light.

15.

17.

knew of his nocturnal ramblings, but had been paid generously to keep her own counsel on the matter. Besides, she had been in fear of James both from his reputation for violence and by threats he had made. However, now she would tell what she knew as a way of warning to others. I suspect it is more likely that she wishes for revenge for her bruises.

When she heard these sounds, she thought her master must be ill, for it had been a particularly damp and windy night. She listened at his door, out of concern for him – though I suspect pure nosiness – and heard what she called a barbarous chanting, very much like the noises made by the Mystery Players she had heard in Cardiff, when those playing devils were performing. Not like Christian speech at all, but more like beasts who could talk. Jenny said that a sort of quiet went around the small group and all looked at one another as if they knew what she meant, perhaps heard of these noises before. No doubt Sam has told his tale for the price of a drink in the Inn. Mrs Bowen went on to say that she had been never so frightened in all her life when she heard James talking at the same time as these noises. She was afraid that he had a devil in there with him, or some sort of wild creature from America. Then silence. She had strained her ears and had been very quiet. Then came James's voice, loud and angry, although she could not make any sense of the words. He seemed to be asking a question and was in a rage at the answer. The door was flung open and he took hold of her neck and almost throttled her on the spot. His face was black and red, and his mouth dribbled and spat while he muttered odd and foul words. He growled and snapped like a beast and pushed her down the stairs. She got out of the door just as he was running down after her, and was lucky to escape with only a kick. She is staying at the Inn for now, and I have agreed to pay for her keep. No doubt she will be much sought after for her story and will bring a good few folk in to buy Mr Richards' ale.

21ST APRIL 1658

LITTLE HAS BEEN heard of James for a few days. No one dares approach the house, and the graveyard is avoided even in the daytime. How he manages we do not know. I am asked what I know but I can tell them nothing. Perhaps I ought to visit, but I am not keen to approach such a man as he has become. I fear him.

30TH APRIL 1658

OUR PREACHER, Mr Hughes, has returned from Cardiff and called round to see me, expressing great worry at James' behaviour. What did I make of it? I could only answer that I thought my brother was a troubled man who seemed out of his wits, and that I have cautioned folk not to approach him. Mr Hughes then came to James' odd language and said he felt most uneasy about it. He has heard of such cases and insanity does not provide a full explanation. He begged me to go with him to the churchyard tonight after dusk falls and I reluctantly agreed.

1ST MAY 1658

WHAT WE SAW last night I can still hardly credit. We got as close as we could to where James was walking. It was a moonless night and we were well disguised in dark clothes. James was wrapped in his cloak and had his arms tight around himself. His eyes were closed, and his teeth and face twisted up as if he were in great pain. He was nodding and chanting. I could make no sense of his words. As he spoke, a low guttural voice came from under the soil. It was as if a dead voice had spoken, dry and rotten. Mr Hughes was pale but determined-looking, and nodded at me as if what he had heard had decided something. We sat silently until James had moved on and then left ourselves.

Back at my house I found to my shame that I was shaking, and I nearly fell into the fire. Mr Hughes held me up and made me drink a brandy, all the time chafing my hands and talking softly to me. 'It is as I feared, David. He is a lost man unless we can help him. I believe that he is in congress with an evil spirit, though how and why I do not know as I cannot understand what he...or it...is saying. Perhaps some language of the Americas. You said he had been near Jamestown? The meeting in Cardiff was to hear news from there, and of the customs our settlers have seen. I believe that he may have delved deeper than a Christian man ought to into what may be called the 'magic' of that area. Its native people

practice wisdom, and keep away from the evil I suspect. I know a man of learning who may help us.'

After he left, I stayed awake until dawn, torn between returning to my brother and my own cowardice.

4TH MAY 1658

MR HUGHES has returned from Cardiff with a Mr Tavish. As part of his mission in Virginia, Mr Tavish has become knowledgeable in the old wisdom and ways of the native people there. We sat in my parlour before setting out, and he told me tales of mischievous or evil spirits that are believed controllable if the correct sacrifices and responses are made. He had spent much effort in telling the people that it is forbidden by God to consort with such beings. Nevertheless, some still did. I asked did he not believe in the power of God? He did, he said, but if foolish men were determined to hand themselves over to darkness nothing would stop them. It was believed that they could only exist in their own land, and my brother must have hoped to escape by coming back to his birthplace, but it had not worked. James was in the grip of a most powerful and evil master. It was our duty to try to save him. We prayed for strength and then at about seven o'clock, before dusk had fallen, we walked up to James' house – watched, I am sure, by the entire village, silent and waiting. It seemed to me that even the birds were quiet, holding back their joyful evening songs as we approached, and I felt that someone in the house was aware of us and was making ready. I do not think that I have ever felt such fear before.

We thudded on the door, but no answer or sound came to us. I called up to James, demanding that he let us in. Nothing. Then it came. The scream. Like a creature in terrible agony, high and so sharp that we had to cover our ears. Then it fell to a groaning voice, which I knew to be my brother's. I was sickened. We stood like three blocks, unable to move.

Coming to ourselves we forced the door in and ran upstairs to where the sounds had come from: James' room. He was on his black oak bed, dead. I will not write the details of what his face and neck were like. I nearly fainted, but Mr

Hughes and Mr Tavish sat me outside the room. They examined him, seeming to know what they were looking for. When they gathered me up and took me out into the warm evening air, the birds were singing. And I wept.

9TH MAY 1658

THE INQUEST has been completed. Visitation of God was the verdict. The details of his injuries have been kept back, as it is feared that otherwise murder may be suspected, and we were glad that we were seen outside the house when the cry was heard. He will be buried tomorrow. Mr Hughes has allowed him to be buried in the churchyard so there should be no unpleasant talk. The story is that he was disturbed in his mind and that he died in a fit.

10TH MAY 1658

THE FUNERAL is over, and a more cheerful air fills the village. I cannot help feeling sad that James' life was so wasted, and I cannot think of any action of his that was kindly, or which did not benefit himself in some way. It is a hard thought, but I am glad that he is dead.

Later I called at Mr Hughes' house. Mr Tavish was also there, and they looked gravely at me as I sat down. They had found a letter from James to me. They suspected that it might be difficult for me to read and asked if I would like them to stay. I agreed. Herein is the letter:

DAVID,

MY BROTHER, I have little time to write this and so must brief. There is little love between us I know, but I beg that you will think less harshly of me after you have read this. I have sinned and am now being punished. Pray for my soul. You know that I went to Virginia when I left Wales. I went about there as a medicine man, using the education our father gave us. Most of my potions and advice worked, and for a time I did well. Then I fell into bad ways again, and lost at gambling. I was hard pressed to pay my debts but on the fourth of May 1653 – a date I will always curse – an old native man told me of an old way of gaining wealth. I was to go to a certain part of the forest and pray to the ancient spirits there, calling one in particu-

lar by its name. If I was favoured, then I would soon be granted my desire. I thought it was nonsense, but I had been drinking and was at my wits' end. I lay down on the wet forest floor and used the words he had told me. As I lay there, I felt above me a swooping and a great movement in the trees. Then came a noise, not quite a voice, which was as cold and dry as a winter wind. It said that I had been granted my wish but that I must one day pay the price for it. I must have passed into unconsciousness or fallen asleep, for I awoke when it was dark. I went back to the town and I heard that the man to whom I owed money had been killed hunting. I was exultant at my good fortune, but not inclined to believe that it had anything to do with the spirits. Later, other things happened that made me rethink. A customer of mine, a rich woman, died and left me a house and gold. Upon packing up at one town, I found a bag of coins under my stall, where no one could have reached. I sold the house and bought a chemist and general store and continued to prosper. I had given little thought to my experience in the forest as everything that increased my wealth could have been down to good luck. I soon knew better.

They say that around there that the native people cursed the land when they were forced out of it, and that some of them set evil spirits to trap and fool the white settlers. I believe the old native man had done just that to me, and I found out later that his son had been killed by some settlers. Then, a year to the day, the voice from the forest spoke again. This time it was angry. It claimed that I had tricked it, that I was not of the tribe it served, and it would punish me for my sacrilege. My God, how it punished me, for it told me the very date I would die: the fourth of May 1658, just before dusk. Does any man wish to know such a thing? After that I was always followed by this terrible being. It talked to me all night and I knew it would never let me go until my death. I thought about killing myself, but as bad a man as I am, I could not do it. I decided to leave America and return to Wales, perhaps going over such a large body of water and returning to my birthplace might throw it off. I sold all I had and took a ship leaving for Portsmouth. In the day I was free of it, but at night the voice was in my head again,

whispering and cursing me and reminding me of the date on which I would die, then less than four years away. I tried reasoning with it and begged it to leave me, but I may as well have tried reasoning with the sea itself. I wish now that I had thrown myself into the waves and been done with it, but every time I got near to doing that something held me back. The thing would not allow it. I must not die until the date it had decided upon. When I got to Wales, I stayed for a while at Cardiff and read what I could about the ways of its own soil, and learnt symbols and magic in an attempt to ward it off. I bought a bed, as one book advised, and carved wheel symbols above where my head would rest. I cut a picture of myself crudely into the wood, as this was meant to distract the spirit from my own body, and a series of lines intended to be a pathway away from me. Nothing worked.

When I returned home to St Fagans I was downhearted to be rejected. I am a wretch and a wicked man, but I had a great need for my brother. I foolishly turned sulky and proud with you. My mind was becoming more and more fogged with the voice calling at me all night and keeping me from rest. I took the house near the churchyard in the hope that the spirit could not touch me there, and to keep myself away from you and your family. I was wrong again. It has no fear of any of our Christian ways. Neither holy ground nor water, nor the cross nor prayer, work against it, nor do these things I have carved into my bed. At night I walk in the yard and it talks to me. I plead with it, but it will not be turned aside. The spirit has control of me. I have seen the body that used to be mine beat an old woman and frighten a man. I am damned and there is no end to it except death. I am writing this on the afternoon of the fourth of May. It will take me soon after dusk. It is a merciless thing. Pray for me, brother.

James.

I read this aloud to Mr Hughes and Mr Tavish. Then it was good to sit with them in the clear evening air and talk of what we saw. They insist that the danger has now gone, and that James is now at rest. I do not know.

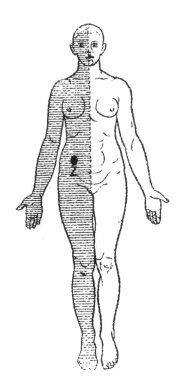

WHERE THE WATERS MEET

BY LUCY ASHE

The twin girls should have been safe, asleep together on the rug by the water. One more day bricking around the mouth of the tunnel and then Samuel could rest. He could go home and bounce his babies on his knee, without worrying about the dust and dirt that followed him from work. His wife would have never let this happen, but she was dead, so it was up to him now.

WHEN HE CLIMBED down from the bridge, he could hear his daughter screaming. He could tell which of them it was before he turned around: she had a desperate wail, impossible to ignore. Serena would join in soon, a duet of cries that he was powerless to calm. A few more steps down the ladder, then she would start. But no second scream came, no piercing squeal syncopated between her sister's lower notes. He turned, looking quickly to the rug where he had left his daughters.

Her sister was shrieking in protest. Serena had vanished.

The men searched for hours, until the last rays of light filtered out and the shadows blended into the night. Women from the nearby cottages joined, their hearts beating painfully in their chests as they glanced over at the widower, Samuel, who had been trying his best for weeks.

When the tunnel opened the next day, Samuel stood above the bridge that he had worked for months to build, holding his lone baby to his chest. She slept fitfully in his arms, reaching out for her sister who was no longer there. Eleven o'clock in the morning, the first day in August, 1820. A parade of boats emerged out from the dark throat of the tunnel into the glare of sunlight, men standing and stretching after 960 yards of walking their feet upside down along the canal roof, from Muriel Street to Duncan Terrace. A crowd had formed. They were blind to Samuel's loss, their cheers drowned out by the brass band and gun salute that celebrated the opening. Samuel turned away and took his daughter home.

LANA RUNS along the canal path every day, in every weather. She runs when it is light and when it is dark. She has no need for a head torch anymore; every step is familiar. If she misses a day, she feels angry, frustrated, like there is an itch that cannot be satisfied. Following the line of the still waters calms her. The direction is a certainty. The only decision is when she must turn around, and usually the Limehouse Basin decides it for her, the labyrinth of paths and roads bringing her

Lana fears these creatures that threaten to take over her body. They arrived one night, erupting inside her without her permission. The man, the father, is faceless, a blank from a night that should not have happened. She has erased him as unimportant, buried him in the darkest corners of the canal.

reluctantly back to the ground. When the sun is behind her, she likes watching her shadow running solidly a few steps in front, leading her onwards. She has never found other people easy, but when she runs on the canal she has a simple, sure feeling of being alone without loneliness. When she runs on the canal, her skin settles over her bones, like a broken vase, patched and filled.

Recently she has felt that pull to the canal more than ever, a drive that makes her fingers fly as she ties up her laces. Her parents worry about her, beg her to take her phone when she runs alone, to stick to the streets with their bright lights after dark. But she dismisses their fears. They have always fussed over her, their only child. Her twin sister is a faint ghost, lost before seeing daylight. Her mother had given birth to Lana first, and then had suffered again, for hours, while her sister, already gone, resisted leaving her mother's womb. The tiny corpse had stuck, like fresh bones too heavy for the grave robber, weighed into the soil. Lana thought of her often and those nine months when they had shared everything in their watery grotto: but Lana had taken too much, leaving her sister to die.

And now Lana, too, is expecting twins. They swim inside her, floating and ducking, like the mare's tail roots that drift through the canal. She has told no-one, only the canal, under the bridge at Haggerston one night at midnight where she screamed her sorrow to the green fingers that sway, mermaid-like, in the dark water. Lana fears these creatures that threaten to take over her body. They arrived one night, erupting inside her without her permission. The man, the father, is faceless, a blank from a night that should not have happened. She has erased him as unimportant, buried him in the darkest corners of the canal.

Saturday, the first day in August. Her mind is at the canal before she has risen from her bed and felt the slow breath of her stomach that she cannot control. She is twenty years old, twenty for the year 2020. Yesterday she went to the hospital alone for her twelve-week scan. The nurse handed her leaflets, numbers to call, a note of concern drafted around the edge of her eyes. Was anyone coming to meet her here? Lana had turned her head slowly, indifferently, to the screen, watching the two creatures shimmer and shake in black and white. Ultrasound: she had imagined its music travelling through her to the water, ultramarine waves, calling up the sea-monsters and mermaids, the canal people who drift across the muddy concrete bottoms. Maybe they would steal them away, changeling babies, brought up like feral watery nymphs.

When she reaches Duncan Terrace Gardens and drops down to the canal path, she tenses. There are too many people crowding her path, blocking her stride with their plastic glasses of beer and cider, their loud cheers, their huge bunches of fiercely-brilliant flowers that girls in dungarees hold too proudly. She frowns. The flower market on Columbia Road must be open again. A band is playing from a barge in City Road Basin. Two-hundred years on, she sighs. She should have avoided the canal today, but she'd forgotten. The canal's birthday, but her birthday too. And why should she let these fair-weather tourists steal her route. The people are an assault, their voices, sunglasses, clothes, flowers, drinks, all too big. She pushes through them, the bodies thick across her path, blocking her shadow from touching on to the water. She can barely breathe. She needs to see into the murky shallows, to glimpse the green weeds that blindly search forwards, colonising the cans, bottles, rusted bike frames that have settled to the bottom.

Finally, the crowd thins to a trickle. She can see the ground again, hear her breath as she dips her head to pass through the bridge under the A-road. She feels the pull of the water, the dark shadows guiding her onwards, shapes drifting in and out of the weeds, a slow ripple of energy. She pauses opposite the gas containers. She has always liked them, big open cages that mark her landscape, certify her belonging. Running has become harder recently; she can feel them like two seahorses turning and twisting inside her. In her shorts, she carries a tiny copy of the scan, a printed scrap that her sweat has crumpled, wrinkling the edges to her skin. She peels it off her damp stomach and glares at it, staring into the shadows of grey shapes that seem to swim in front of her eyes.

A movement in the water lifts her gaze from

At first, Lana thinks she is looking at herself, reflected back in the still surface of the canal. But there is something different, she thinks, when she looks harder and the water refuses to dissolve and form as she moves. Her hair: in the water, it is billowing in and out of the reeds. But Lana's hair is tied up above her head.

the scan. She moves closer and peers down. The water is clear, a rare patch cleansed, empty of rubbish, just a few reeds and roots from the water violet reaching down through the shallow mirror. At first, Lana thinks she is looking at herself, reflected back in the still surface of the canal. But there is something different, she thinks, when she looks harder and the water refuses to dissolve and form as she moves. Her hair: in the water, it is billowing in and out of the reeds. But Lana's hair is tied up above her head. She reaches up, instinctively, to check, but the hand in the water does not match hers. Instead, another hand, white and translucent, shoots out of the water towards her, and then is gone. Lana gasps and pushes back against the tow-path wall, breathing hard. Slowly, she inches closer again, oblivious to how she must look to the passers-by on their bikes. As she glances down once again, the creature turns and vanishes. The water ripples before it re-settles on Lana's face, certainly her face this time.

When she gets home, still breathless, she realises her scan has gone. She doesn't remember dropping it, but she must have done. She closes her eyes and tries to remember what happened. Did she drop it in the water, giving up those two swelling, fluttering shapes to the figure, the mermaid, the reflection, that haunts her?

IT WILL BE a cold February, ice collecting in patches across the surface of the canal. Lana will give birth to one child: she will name her Serena, her siren sending her back to the canal before the nurses have even signed the forms. The other twin, she will be lost, vanished, stolen from Lana's swollen body. The twenty-week scan reveals a single creature, alone, floating in her womb like a water nymph. Lana will return to the canal every day, hunting along the water, in the reeds, in the tumbling brick walls around the throats of the tunnels, for the echo who stole her daughter. One day she will find her. She will search in the shallows under Haggerston Bridge and there they will be. Two women, their hair tangled in the reeds, playing in the shadows of the canal.

DEVIL IN MY EYE

BY K. M. HAZEL

Franklin accepted that it was now impossible to reach the Salvation Army hostel in Walsall before it closed its doors at nine p.m. He had been a fool to attempt the journey on foot in these conditions. Snow had been falling fast since midday and there seemed no prospect of the blizzard ending.

HE HAD HOPED to spend Christmas with his eldest sister and her husband. Though the rest of his family regarded him as the proverbial bad penny, Helen had always done her best to make him feel welcome. But in the two years since he had last seen her, Helen and Tom had moved on. They had left no forwarding address with the old man who now occupied their former cottage, leaving Franklin to conclude that even his most loyal sibling had now turned her back on him. At least the codger had sent him away bearing half a loaf of stale bread, a lump of hard cheese, and directions to the hostel.

Tracts of farmland lay between Franklin and the most direct route into Walsall. The old man's garbled instructions had taken Franklin into a maze of narrow lanes whose similarity had combined with poor visibility to convince him he had been walking in circles for the last hour. The lack of road signs proved equally puzzling. Franklin wondered if the local authority had simply failed to replace the ones removed during wartime.

Around the next bend, an answer to his problems presented itself in the form of a sign nailed to an elm tree beside a turn-off in the lane. The lone marker vanished almost instantly as the wind whipped up a screen of churning snowflakes. After the squall had passed, Franklin moved close enough to read the message on the elaborately carved sign.

VISIT BOYTON'S FARM. EGGS, MILK AND BACON FOR SALE.
BEST IN THE BLACK COUNTRY!

The suggestion of food made Franklin's stomach growl with hunger. But it was the dozen or more tramps' marks scratched into the bark of the tree that really excited his interest. The marks informed anyone familiar with the vagabond's code that a sit-down meal might be on offer at the farm.

A finger-shaped protuberance on one end of the sign pointed down a narrow track that sloped away between tall hawthorn hedges.

Franklin decided that he had no real alternative but to avail himself of Mr Boyton's charity. His old army kit bag felt like a sack of coal on his aching back, but his hands were too stiff

with cold to do more than allow the cumbersome weight to hang off his lank frame by a strap of fraying rope. Pushing unfeeling fingers into his overcoat pockets, Franklin set off down the winding track, grateful for the respite from the wind provided by the thorny arbour.

The track ended after a quarter of a mile at a five-bar gate fortified by a rusting padlock. Through the swirling snow, Franklin made out a small whitewashed farmhouse at the back of a yard fringed by a variety of outbuildings. No light gleamed in the windows visible on this side of the house, and though it was impossible to be certain at this distance, he could detect no wisp of smoke from the chimney. Hardly the welcoming Yuletide haven he had envisaged on his way down the meandering track.

An open door began to slam beyond the whirling dotted curtain that danced before his watering eyes. The first sharp retort caused him to jump back and almost lose his footing on the rutted ground beneath the snow.

As he silently cursed his skittishness, he listened for the sounds of restive livestock and for any indication that the banging door had disturbed the residents of the farmhouse. He detected no signs of life. It seemed he had stumbled across an abandoned dwelling – a rare thing in a post-war England humbled by austerity.

As he clambered over the gate, Franklin noticed another tramp's mark on the gatepost that told him he had reached a place of safety.

He waded through knee-deep snow in the yard and slipped the bolt on the upper half of a flapping paddock door. Moving to the house, he peered through a kitchen windowpane glazed with ice. In the dimness beyond, he saw a bulky object on the table that his straining eyes could not resolve into anything definite. Directly opposite the window was a Welsh dresser devoid of crockery save for a baffling fragment of Blue Willow plate on a hardwood stand.

Franklin tried the back door and found it unlocked.

The remains of a decorative dinner service crunched underfoot as he made a habitually-cautious entrance. A rank smell emanated from the greasy stove and mingled with various odours of decay to curdle his grumbling stomach. The item on the table proved to be an

enormous family Bible wrapped in a crocheted shawl. He opened the cracked leather binding to a copperplate list of Boyton family members spanning five generations. The line of succession appeared to end with John and Mary Boyton, the children of Isaac and Elizabeth.

A bulge in the page betrayed the presence of an object between subsequent gilt-edged leaves. Franklin turned to the relevant section and revealed a penknife with a fine tortoiseshell handle seemingly acting as a page marker. He read the passage from Revelation underlined by the extended blade.

'Then the beast was captured, and with him the false prophet who worked signs in his presence, by which he deceived those who received the mark of the beast and those who worshiped his image.'

Franklin spat on the page in disgust. He had sat through countless sermons merely to fill his belly, but the well-meaning efforts of do-gooders had left him with little fondness for improving works.

He folded the knife and placed it in his overcoat pocket. Leaving his kit bag propped against the back door, he left the kitchen and entered a passage lined with photographs.

Gloom shrouded the finer details in the pictures, all of which hung askew in frames with spiderweb cracks in their glass.

He found a parlour at the end of the passage and opened its curtains to admit the snow's reflected light. A lane ran past the farm on this side of the house. Beyond lay a field that glowed beneath a turbulent sky as it rose towards a distant copse. The wind had dropped, and the snow now fell with soothing calmness, as if suspended in liquid. A profound silence ('a country silence,' his mother would have called it) seemed to hold Franklin spellbound for a moment. He realised that he was listening for something the wind had previously masked but could not for the life of him have said what.

He shook his head to dispel the peculiar enchantment then turned from the window.

Compared to the kitchen, the parlour was in good order. There was coal in the scuttle and a cord of firewood gathering dust on the cast-iron hearth. The one obvious sign of vandalism was the destruction of a painting that had obviously hung above the fireplace: burned fragments of the picture had survived among the ashes in the grate.

Franklin examined the pile of newspapers

beside the scuttle. The local rags were pre-war. December 15, 1938 was the most recent date on the yellowing newsprint.

Almost sixteen years ago to the day…

It did not seem likely, Franklin reasoned, that the war had robbed the farm of men. A domestic tragedy of some kind must have made the farm untenable.

The band of outcasts he had reluctantly joined often shared spook tales, but Franklin had never heard Boyton's Farm mentioned in this context. He pushed thoughts of haunted houses to the back of his mind. He was neither a child nor a simpleton and there was nothing here he need fear. Yet there was no doubt that an atmosphere of intense melancholy seemed to permeate this desolate place: he had sensed it the moment he had touched the Bible.

Franklin lit the paraffin lamp on the mantle with one of his five remaining matches, then wasted no more time in getting a fire started. He spent ten blissful minutes thawing his feet in front of the resulting blaze, after which he left his boots and socks steaming on the hearth while he investigated the rest of the house.

Twelve steps adorned by a dark red runner took him to the upstairs landing. At the summit, Franklin saw that a previous visitor had scratched an obscure symbol into the wall facing the stairs. The tramp had made his mark in the faded rectangle where a picture had once hung, placing the strokes with such reckless pressure that they had cut into the plaster beneath the pale-yellow wallpaper. Franklin was unable to decipher the sign, which resembled a crude eye that seemed to shimmer in the guttering lamplight.

The lamp revealed a hallway with four open doors, at the end of which a leaded window gleamed with effulgent light. The threadbare runner continued along the passage, traversing varnished boards furred by dust. Cobwebs festooned the low ceiling, forcing him to duck as he moved to the first door.

He did little more than glance inside. A tiny bed, stripped to its wooden frame, stood against the wall beneath a sampler embroidered with the dictum 'honour thy father and thy mother'. The bed's ornate headboard reminded him of the sign on the elm tree: the same skilled hand had clearly crafted both.

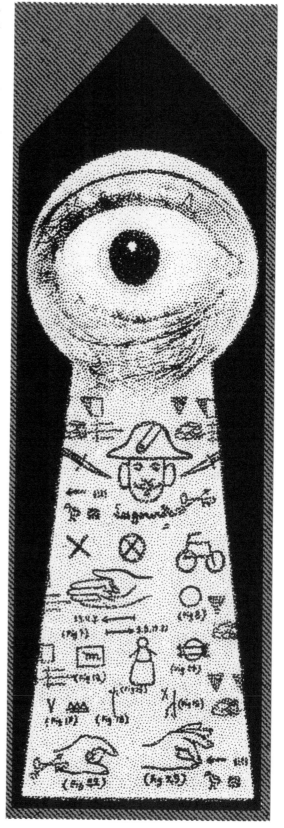

The next door showed him another child's bedroom. Books bloated by damp lay scattered across bare floorboards. A one-armed doll sat on the denuded bed, smiling as if it had been waiting for him.

Nothing but rodent droppings lined the shelves of the adjacent linen closet.

He moved to the final room, his bare feet numb with cold once more, and found a scene of utter devastation. He stepped over the threshold, shuddering as a dangling cobweb fondled his scalp. A toppled chest of drawers lay among its broken innards and strewn contents. A chamber pot peeped from beneath the stripped bedframe, miraculously intact amongst the fragments of a dressing table mirror that littered the bedside rug. Something like a hatchet had all but obliterated the decorative carving on the mahogany headboard of the double bed. The same implement might also have defaced the walls, Franklin thought. Scratched like ragged hieroglyphics into seemingly every inch of florid wallpaper was a bewildering sequence of symbols.

Franklin picked out the more obvious tramp signs, but ninety percent of the markings conveyed no meaning to him besides the evident derangement of their author. Madness was a common character trait among the unfortunates Franklin had encountered on his travels. The open road was an asylum that ordinary people rarely visited, and it led inevitably to darkness and tragedy.

Franklin returned to the sitting room. He waited until his socks and boots were dry, then collected enough coal from the yard to keep the fire burning all night.

Snow was still falling. An animal howled mournfully somewhere in the arctic wilderness, perhaps in response to the whistling wind.

After barricading the back door with the kitchen table, an exhausted Franklin settled down for the night. He boiled snow on the hearth to make cocoa, using up the last of his ration. He drank this with a meal consisting of the old man's bread and cheese then fell into a contented slumber in the armchair by the fire.

He awoke in the small hours to the renewed slamming of the paddock door. With a resigned sigh, he slipped on his boots and overcoat and carried the lamp to the front door. He was pleased to see a large iron key poking from the lock, which he turned with a protesting screech. Leaving the lamp on the hall table, he plunged into the freshly risen gale.

Franklin noted that the paddock door was ill-fitting and prone to vibration. He reasoned that the wind had shaken the bolt free as he secured it once more.

At least the snow had stopped for the moment.

As he fled back to the house, his teeth clattering in the raw air, he saw that the deranged vandal who had defaced the bedroom had also marked the lower panel of the front door in his signature style.

Franklin bent to examine the carving.

The mark was both old and new, he observed. A different blade had followed the lines of an existing design, as if to renew its power...but he was alarming himself unnecessarily – the second draft was undoubtedly years old. Despite this reassurance, the discovery had struck his mind with a sickening jolt. George Lambert, the veteran tramp who had taught him the meaning of the signs, had called the one on the door 'the black spot' after the device in *Treasure Island*. The sign consisted of two vertical lines in a circle inset with dots denoting the evil eye. The mark was a corruption of one of the many vagrant signs for danger: its literal meaning was 'vengeance is mine'. Franklin had last seen the mark daubed above the doss house bed of a pickpocket whose throat someone had cut in the night.

A prickling on the back of his neck made Franklin rise from his crouch and turn uneasily.

He saw what had raised his hackles standing at the top of the field beyond the now impassable lane. No features were discernible on the distant figure who resembled, Franklin thought, a dead fly on a linen tablecloth in the vastness of the snowbound field.

Franklin called out a warning to the stranger.

His outburst caused a flurry of snow to cascade down from the roof and land harmlessly beside him. When Franklin looked again at the watcher, it seemed that he had moved indefinably closer. Unnerved, Franklin stepped back into the house.

His mentor had once told him the story of the Eternal Wanderer, an evil spirit said to appear when a man 'on the tramp' was at his lowest ebb. Was this a devil come to do him harm or merely the kind of earthly menace he had faced a hundred times before?

Franklin had never been much of a fighter. The war had been kind to him and the only man he had ever killed in anger had become his victim during the first heady months of peacetime. An argument over a woman. A foolish and entitled act, and the reason he had spent years running from the hangman's noose.

He pushed the door shut, panicking for a moment when its lower edge snagged on an uneven floor tile. With the door securely locked, he felt confident that he had set an unbreachable barrier between himself and any immediate danger.

He grabbed the lamp from the hall table. As he turned to enter the sitting room, he froze.

Framed by the kitchen doorway was the outline of a man. No sound had announced the intruder's entrance, Franklin realised with mounting dread. He angled the lamp and highlighted what looked like a shadow loosed from its human mooring. The features of the former man appeared as gradations of darkness atop a suggestion of ragged clothing. Its eyes alone were clearly discernible: wide and unblinking and stark white in the greater blackness, the holes at their centre trembling. The thing reeked of every unwashed body Franklin had ever slept beside. The stench suggested the leprous corruption of a rotting soul to his appalled mind.

Smiling with its eyes, the thing raised the billhook clutched in its rudimentary hand.

Having nowhere else to run, Franklin darted up the stairs.

He stumbled backwards past the rooms on the upper landing as his pursuer advanced with calculated slowness. The first bedroom was as he remembered it, but in the second, the doll on the bed had become a little girl sketching on a slate with chalk. Her beckoning smile mimicked the dryly pulsing wound in her throat.

The thing scraped the billhook against the wall to regain Franklin's attention. But the sense of another unnatural presence again forced Franklin to look away. A terrified child – a boy this time – touched a finger to his lips, imploring with nothing but empty eye sockets for Franklin to keep the secret of his hiding place in the linen closet. The master bedroom held even greater horrors. Here, a man and a woman lay sprawled on the bed, their heads little more than red stains on shredded straw pillows.

Franklin screamed in pity and fear.

In reply, demented laughter rippled in an echoing loop throughout the house. The thing drew signs in the air with the billhook as it toyed with its prey. The black spot, Franklin read, his panicked eyes following the tip of the blade as it carved the foetid air.

He could not allow the thing to etch the sign into unresisting flesh.

The billhook reminded him of the penknife he had taken from the Bible. Fishing the knife from his pocket, he opened the blade with his teeth.

Suspicion flared in the thing's gleaming eyes as Franklin fell into a crouch and made a mark in the runner with barely-controlled slashes of the knife.

He retreated to the end of the landing and watched the thing hover behind his near illegible sign, its lamplight eyes becoming beacons of hatred. It could not pass, Franklin saw with relief. Thank God he had paid attention all those years ago when George had shown him a sign that bestowed protection on the road. George had carried the same mark on a scrap of paper in his hat until his dying day.

Franklin yanked open the leaded casement. The wind gusted in and set cobwebs dancing along the passage. The incoming air smelled clean and vital after the foulness the thing had carried into the house.

The farm's other tenants had joined their murderer behind the protective symbol. They looked now as they had done in life and impressed upon Franklin an understanding that the farmhouse was a trap he could not allow other lost souls to blunder into.

With a nod to the gentle farmer who had invited this nightmare into his life, Franklin hurled the lamp.

Paraffin spilled in a fiery circle around the apparition. The thing shrieked with frustration, an agonising cacophony that dropped Franklin to his knees as the conflagration spread rapidly to the walls.

A recovered Franklin barely had time to plunge through the window before licking flames chased him out. The roof of the coal shed broke his fall. He rose after a second bounce, dazed but unharmed, from the yard's deep carpet of snow.

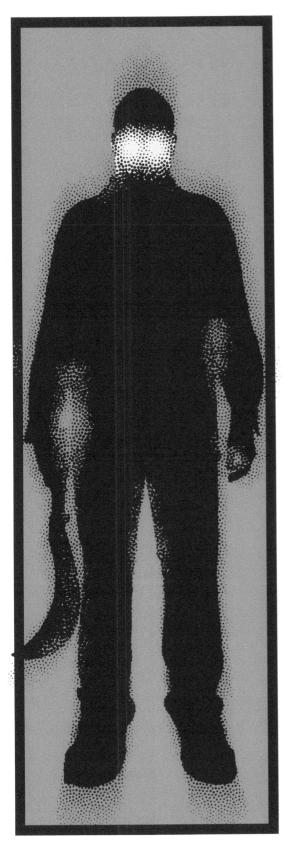

He watched the house burn from the lane, awed by the speed with which the fire established its destructive dominion.

Franklin arrived at the hostel five minutes before closing time. To his great relief, a place had unexpectedly become available. As the elderly warden escorted him to his room, Franklin could not resist asking him what he knew about Boyton's Farm.

'Harold Rudd was the last tramp to enjoy Boyton's hospitality,' the warden explained after warming to his tale. 'The family was never known to turn away a hungry man, and so they made Rudd welcome when he turned up at their door.

'Rudd was a fixture at our hostel back then. He'd been a scholar of sorts in his day but had lost his reason and position in the wrong kind of books. Obsessed with symbols was Harold. Always seemed to be writing in the air with his finger. 'Protection,' he called it.

'Well, Isaac Boyton had a little girl. The child gave Rudd a drawing she'd done of him. Perfectly innocent, you would think. But Rudd – such was the twist in his brain – saw something sinister in the picture and accused the family of trying to put the Devil in him. He said as much in the note he left after doing away with himself. You see, Rudd believed the Devil lurked wherever the eye might let him in; and believing something *had* got into him through the drawing, he took his revenge. Still gives me a shiver to think of it.'

The warden handed Franklin a coarse blanket and gestured towards a rickety camp bed with a stained mattress.

'Rudd is the reason you've got somewhere to lay your head tonight. The regulars here who knew Harold often claim to see his ghost. The daft bugger whose place you've taken is one of them. Told me he'd seen Rudd making signs over the bed I'd allocated him. Said he'd sooner sleep in the street than take what belonged to a dead man. His loss is your gain, I suppose...'

FIRSTBORN

BY DAMIEN B. RAPHAEL

The **night** Father offers me
to the witch, he drags me
from my bed and marches me
through the forest, barefoot. I
slip and curse, whimpering when my toes
catch on roots of dead ash.

'**N**O MORE of that, boy,' Father says, bringing his lantern an inch from my nightcap. 'You're halfway a man. Don't falter now.' I nod through a smudge of tears and Father leads me on, his stout hand trapping the pulse of fear in my wrist. There's a grit of muck-sweat along his rough skin, and it's welcome – though I don't be telling him that. Twice he's hugged me in my life. I count this as the third, and the last. The luckiest.

Most folk say the forest belongs to her, the wise woman of Wychwood, and her alone. They are wrong. It belongs to our offerings made of bone and blood and heartache. To Sally Payne, drunk on dwale and tricked into sleep. To little Robin Fletcher with his picnic of kale and mangold and baskets of medlars, too young and full bellied to remember his way home.

And now, this night, to me.

We soon find the trail, a path of moss found only by those who desire to meet her. The change is welcome. Soft, warm and waterlogged. Like velvet under my ashen feet. Some folk search from cherry time to cherry time without so much as a sniff, so Father says. Yet his words don't bring me comfort, for he halts mid-sentence at something beyond the sloping beechwoods and my heart thunders. Firstly, there's the cottage. Worts Well cottage. Best never spoken of, and then only in whispers. Its tiled roof has crumpled in places, ivy and fungus – King Alfred's cakes – spotting its buttery stonework.

Father isn't looking at the hovel, though.

Raking through the mist are new tines crowning the skulls of stags. A herd of them. Skulking past us, their antlers are livid with blood, as if daubed in ripe figs – the shedding of their baby skin. They circle the cottage like a living fence. A shield of sinew and fur.

It's enough for Father. He shucks the rope off his shoulders, and points to a hedge maple. The skirt of its leaves scratches my head as I walk to the trunk, and Father follows, crouching as he ties me to it. He does this slow and careful, but the cinching of the knot cuts under my rib. A sigh slips out and I begin to pant, afraid. Father offers no words to quell my fear. Instead, he pulls out something from inside his thrift, a gimcrack necklace he bought for Mother from a travelling hawker, and loops it around my head.

'You hold true to the bargain, Ann Hemings,' Fathers says, facing the ruin. 'It's a fine sacrifice. Be merciful, be quick.'

I don't blame him for using the rope. Everyone does. They have to. Ever since that hedger lad came stumbling back to the village, shivering, and frothing, and acting out. When the priest blessed him, he spat and screeched like a cat. Rope was the cure, it seemed. To bind the madness deep in the woods. And with it the witch.

It's said Ann Hemings appeared when all the corn was in stacks, walking through the village with a charmed grace, her silken skirt damp with morning dew. She carried her daughter on her hip, set herself up in a cow-house long since abandoned, telling fortunes under fat golden moons. People flocked to her, such was her gift. Most were glad their coins parted on good news. But some turned grudgeful at their supposed misfortunes, and their whisperings of gossip turned to hearsay and threats. Having reaped that ill will, Ann appeared in the square one morning howling with grief, cradling her pale-skinned, rag-doll child. She kicked over flitches of bacon, creels of bread. Demanded her daughter's murderer make themselves known. But no one dared say a peep, and she cursed all who

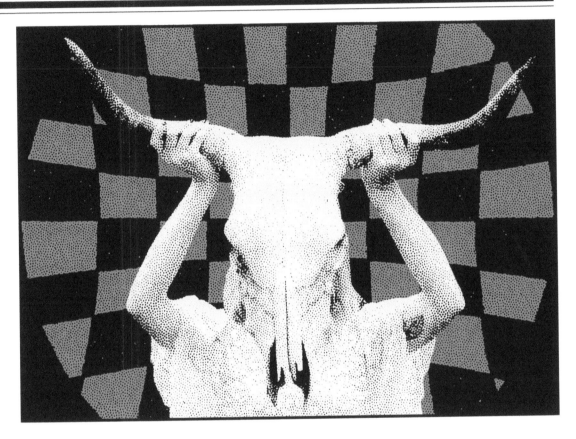

heard her, and even those that couldn't. I asked Mother once what the witch said, after a day of harvesting with her bagging hook. *There's nothing to tell on it, little one. All that witch blustered about was smiting us with fevers if the murderer don't own up. Course no one did, and she demanded our firstborn as penance. But in all those days afterward, we didn't see so much as a pair of dancing mice.*

Five summers ago, that was. Five summers, and now baby sister Aldith, not two months old, has started showing the signs of the fever, the strange spots. Just like all the others. I offered to go, and Mother blinked, her eyes wild.

And the words of protest I longed to hear never came.

I'm dreaming of Mother when I wake from a half sleep, squinting at the cottage.

And she is there, standing in the doorway. The witch.

The thought of how long she's been watching is an ice across my scalp. It crawls down my spine, my legs. Frozen, I study her. Her head is tilted back, bearing a pale, taut throat. Her eyes are pools of swindle. She raises a hand like we're about to go on a walk. Like I'm her child, and the ropes that bind me fall away. When I look again, she steps back into her fold.

I linger on her doorstep.

The darkness within is thick as charred wood, a glut of stillness at every turn. There's a foul smell too, like spoiled meat. Or spoiled life.

She calls to me with a voice like needles, and foxes fighting in the night. Gulping down my fear, I enter and tiptoe across heaving floors, finding her in the parlour. She faces a turf fire, a shadow-shape working a spinning wheel. Stooks of flax surround her. Scutching boards. Hackles. The wheel sounds broken, a constant *skur-skur-skur*. I cannot breathe for it. It sets my teeth on edge.

'Why have you come here, Osric?'

'To save my sister.' And I want to add: from your heathen craft, but lack the courage. 'I volunteered.'

The wheel grinds to a halt, and she sits there, unmoving. 'Punishment does not lie in choice, not for those who are guilty. I am making my dress now. I must hurry.'

She says I am special. That I am not to be enchanted like the others.

Instead, she teaches me the herblore, her lessons always at night. Standing over me whilst I doze, she offers me her hand again, and I leave my body. We fly through the forest, as she shows me herbs to make her simples: foxglove, peppermint, and broom. 'For deafness,' she says, 'ram's piss, eel's bile and the sap of ash trickled into each ear. A gangrenous wound? Smother it with the dung of a bull. A cure for sleeplessness, well, that be poppy heads simmered in wine. Now you tell me, Osric. What is the cure for guilt?'

My tongue is tied, and I cannot answer.

On the sixth day of the moon, she collects mistletoe cut with a sickle and I hold up white cloth to catch the berries – her most cherished yield in all the woodland. Before she culls them, she washes her bare feet in the purest stream and offers her gods a sacrifice of bread and mead. 'I shall make a decoction of mistletoe,' she says, 'and drink until I fit to burst. It makes good for fruitfulness, not just in me, but in all the animals of my forest.'

She boils her ingredients over a pan and my belly grumbles. These past few weeks I've been fed nothing but tea kettle broth: hot water and milk and a dash of salt. Sometimes there's flour and a little butter mixed together for pudding, but that is rare.

One day she leaves me and says she'll return after her business. I think to run away, a thought snuffed out as quick as a flame. How could Father forgive me if I returned, and what of Aldith? What death would await her? I content myself to search around the house.

Most rooms lie empty and rotting. Apart from one. In that backroom the boards lie uneven, curled from rain. Every few paces sit piles of clothes, as if whoever had worn them had merely wriggled free, shedding skin. I peer at a discarded kirtle and it's covered in fur and dried blood, a mildewed poppet left where it fell. I start from a thump.

'Hello?'

Across the room, someone moans. They lay on their side, facing a wall. No taller than I.

Their shoulders and neck are whiter than milk-sop, and twisted wrong, like a blind bonesetter had kneaded them beyond hope and splintered each joint in leather and comfrey root. The skin shines with sweat. A leg kicks out. Such violence to it. Such spite.

I back away and her hands slide up my back, finding the dips above my collarbones. I gasp at the shock of Ann's touch, her sudden presence, the wetness of her salty breath in my ear. 'They do not take to it, sometimes,' she says. 'My familiars. Some are too attached to who they were. Their loved ones. It poisons them. Come, there is work for you.'

She bids me find creatures, the smallest workers of the forest. Beetles, spiders, bees and grubs. 'But you must find them dead from their industry,' she says. 'Nothing harmed, no matter how small.'

The freedom from the cottage is delicious. The first day, I walk for miles, dizzy on elder blossom, clambering over loose bricked walls. And when I chance on a patch of cow parsley, I fall clean asleep, the sun too hot and charming.

When I return to the cottage, it's early evening. Worse, I'm empty handed. Sneaking upstairs, my belly lurches at Ann beside my bed of rushes, arms locked by her side, fingers splayed. Watching. Apologies don't sway her, and the crushing silence snakes around my chest.

At last, she says, 'A man shall visit us soon.'

'Who?' I say, breathing again.

'The one who took my child from me. A coward. Make haste in your work.'

The next day, as if heeding Ann's tongue, the forest floor is littered with pickings. Dragonflies, moths and snail shells. When I hand over my basket full of dead things she nods, pleased.

True to her word, one muggy evening her guest appears. Beside the well, I watch him approach the cottage, trampling a path through a bank of nettles. A longing to be saved kindles in me, even by the hand of a killer.

The more he marches closer, though, the more that hope withers. His movement is too familiar, the gait too bold. The world crumbles to dream, as my numb legs carry me away from the well, swift over bone dry grass.

Swift to meet Father.

'You can't be here,' I say reaching him, my head abuzz. He looks at me, groggy and flushed. He's been drinking, glassy eyed, his lips stained with wild fruit wine. 'You can't be here,' I say again, stupidly. 'She's awaiting the man who killed her child.'

The look he gives me, now. All piss and vinegar and petulance. His guilt may's well be decorated with sprigs of holly, laurel, and yew. I am feeble with realisation.

I cough and splutter. Bash fists against my temples. 'And you let me here to die? Let us all to die?' Father blinks and grinds his teeth, stewing in thought. 'Why, Da?'

He grabs a bunch of my tunic, face sour with venom. 'She told me your mother would spurn me, aye. But worse than that, she said my firstborn would forsake me, too. I don't know which is worse.' Father pushes me to the ground, into dust. 'But it's all for nothing, now. Your sacrifice wasn't worthy. Mother and Aldith are courting death. I'm here to end Ann Heming's rot.'

A cool current of air glances us. We both turn back to the cottage, and the change is irresistible. No longer is it clothed in nightmare, no longer a place of pain. It shimmers under the lavender sky, damask roses clinging to its stones. Gold and pink light leaks from its windows. And in the doorway, combing back a curtain of glass beads, stands Ann herself.

No knotted hair. No leanness. Instead, she glows, olive-skinned and jangling with hoops of silver. Her dress is a marvel, busy with curled ribbons, swan feathers and lace. Its emerald silk has been embroidered with beetles, bronze-threaded moths. All the things I had collected for her. Each spun with glamour.

She holds out her hands, her fingers slim and tender with longing. 'You can still save them,' she says to Father. 'Stay. Repair what was taken.'

The tall grass by the edge of the forest is where I make my bed that night, and when at last sleep drags me under, the dreams are of Ann, her long arms blistering and peeling, spotted with her curse.

Next morning, Father has gone.

The colours of Ann's vision sit heavy in the gut, like a pound of marchpane. And when the glamour fades – its sugar thinning through my blood – the grubbiness of the Earth reclaims her house brick by brick.

My body slows. Becomes unwilling.

I sleep most days past noon, wishing my stillness last forever. Every waking moment is like gulping down bitter spoonfuls of memory. Father, Mother and Aldith. I want to rip them from my thoughts like rotten teeth. Slice them away like a barber-surgeon would a pus-riddled finger. Father most of all.

To see Ann's belly soon swell, round with my half-sister, may's well be ten lashes of blackthorn at my back. With gritted teeth I listen to new instructions, to fetch new herbs for helping the child.

Sometimes, I think I see Father on these errands. A hooded stranger always lurking,

threatening to make himself known. Some-times, I wonder if anyone can see me at all. When he veers too close, I thrash wildflowers with a stick, cursing his name. And when he bolts, I keep lashing out, until the flowers are shredded, their stalks pulped. Until my lungs are fit to burst.

The temptation to throw his necklace into the swamp at the heart of the wood is like a hunger. But each time it comes to it, my heart is too weak. A heart too hollow and made of chalk. Easy to flake. Just like Father's.

My half-sister is born as the Dog Star slips below the horizon. The sound of her wailing, a scythe through the cottage.

I fetch water and moss for Ann to clean the baby, make them comfortable on a prop of straw. All day long, she whispers incantations and draws symbols on the baby's scalp, her fingers glistening with yarrow oil, dipped in crushed cloves. The child quietens then, content to watch the dried fruits I'd strung together with red thread, swaying from the rafters.

When I catch a thin smile on Ann's lips I leave them, and walk until my calves are fire, to

find the crevice of a tree trunk, the oldest knotted oak in the middle of the wood. I climb inside its mossy belly and stay there until the moon's bloodless light lays a speckled path through the boughs outside, and dream of being reborn with roots for legs and whortleberries for eyes.

The first hoar frost of winter heralds snow. A powder that leeches all sounds from the forest.

It makes it easy to hear their arrival, miles away.

Blood-baited voices, yowling hunting dogs.

I drop my fir cones and firewood and rush like water back to the cottage.

Father is already there, beside Ann and her child in the kitchen. A phoenix of hope rises in my throat, before it's picked apart by Father's words, feather by feather. 'The babe is my blood,' he says. Not me. He says nothing of me.

Ann studies him, her eyes dark and unyielding. 'You led them here,' she says.

The shouting echoes closer. Father does not deny it. Ann brings her crying baby close and whispers to it honeyed promises, before offering the infant to us. Father takes it, and in his calloused hands it falls fast asleep.

Hiding in the shadows, Father and I watch Ann being dragged from her house by men clutching crosses. Both of us too craven to stop it.

There are stories about her fate, from Father and people in town. Half drowned on a ducking stool, then put to fire in the square, until her tongue was too swollen for spells, until her lips had shrivelled back to the gums, her fingers cracked and breaking.

The villagers laugh about such details, and when they do, I sneak away, hurling stones at their windows. To be acting so courts disaster. Suspicions already hover over my head. They say I am the boy who escaped. Unharmed. The others were not so lucky. Returning one by one from the forest, their heads are clouded, wordless.

Father, though, basks in the villagers' pride. He is their champion to have led them to her. To have helped return their children. The local lumbermen offer to rebuild our house. Some days, I sit and watch them saw the timbers in the yard, marking their protective symbols of burns and checkerboard scratches along the beams with their scoop knives. *To snare evil spirits in their webbing*, they say. *To snare witches.*

But that will not help Father. Not whilst I still live there.

I am all but a stranger to him. He dotes over the witch child now, a new obsession. Mother and Aldith may's well be ghosts, banished to an outhouse, their scarred faces wrapped under sackcloth.

Father is all but a ghost too.

When at last the carpenters leave, taking their saws and knives and paste pots, I seize the chance to set things right. I fill Father's nightcup to the brim with freshly brewed poppy wine, and offer it to him before a fire. By midnight he sleeps, deeper than Wort's Well cottage is set in the Wychwood.

I place a shoe in his lap, clogged with mortar – the shoe I'd pulled out from behind the chimney, another protection. But he needn't worry. His room's still safe – the countless daisy wheels carved into the sill beam, the dwarf walls, the cross frames are enough to repel all but a coven. No, the shoe in his lap is from upstairs.

Unhooking the necklace he left me that night in the wood, I lace it around his crooked head. Snag the bunch of keys from his belt.

'Father,' I whisper into his ear, but cannot find the right words.

I lock myself inside the baby's room. Rest my head beside her cot. I do not remember falling asleep, but something tears me from a dreamless chasm. Father's incoherent bellowing. Footsteps, now. Voices. I have made the drink too weak. But the door is solid oak, and should hold fast against ten men. A smell blooms under my nose. Of charred skin, roasted meat. Broken promises. A breath catches in my throat at a sound, a *skur-skur-skur*. I do not turn around to face it. I do not turn around to see what I already know. That Ann is here. Birthed from the chimney. Skin as burnt as toast. Skull as hairless as her babe. She's grown tall, her limbs spindle thin like she's been slipping hud.

The heat of charred skin scratches my neck as she peers over me at the cot. And I want to tell her to take it and be gone, when the stubs of fingers seek my shoulders. The touch is like a question. I can't breathe. She turns to me, her face a roaring fire. And I remember our nights in the forest. Of our freedom, her power. It is too much. I am unstitched in her presence. A coward. Let us fly again, through the Wychwood, she says.

For you are the cure.
Let us fly.

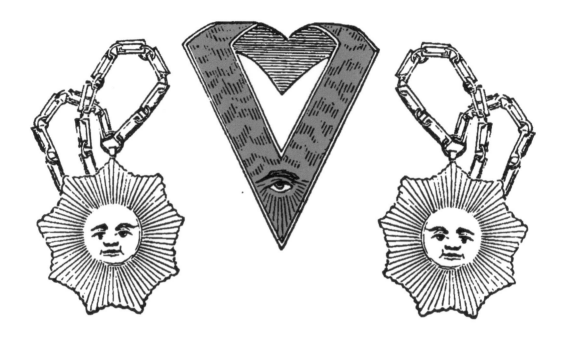

LUCY ASHE is an English teacher. She writes reviews for *Playstosee.com* and currently has a feminist dystopian novel out on submission to agents. Her poetry and prose is soon to be published in *Truffle Literary Magazine* and *192, Poets' Directory*. Twitter: @LSAshe1

BARRY CHARMAN is a writer living in London, England. He has been published in various magazines, including *Ambit*, *Firewords Quarterly*, *Bare Fiction Magazine* and *Popshot Quarterly*. He has had poems published online and in print, most recently in *The Literary Hatchet* and *The Linnet's Wings*. He has a blog at *barrycharman.blogspot.co.uk*

VICTORIA DAY has appeared in the following publications: *Ghosts and Scholars Magazine*, *Nebula Press*, *Vault of Evil*, *Sarob Press*, *A Ghostly Company Newsletter*, *Supernatural Tales* and *The Silent Companion*.

K. M. HAZEL is a graphic designer by profession who lives and works in the Black Country, England. His stories have appeared in *Sanitarium*, *Gorezone*, *Samhain* and the Far Horizons anthology *Forever Hungry*. He is currently working on the first series of a ghost story podcast called *Hobland*, which he hopes to make available early next year.

TOM JOHNSTONE's stories have appeared in publications as *A Ghosts and Scholars Book of Folk Horror* (Sarob Press), *Single Slices* (Cutting Block Press), *Black Static #68* (TTA Press) and *Best Horror of the Year #8* (Night Shade Books), with further anthology appearances scheduled in *Nightscript Vol. 6* (Chthonic Matter Press), *Terror Tales of the Home Counties* (Telos Publications) and *Body Shocks* (Tachyon Publications). Find out more about his writing at *tomjohnstone.wordpress.com*

KRISTY KERRUISH is from Edinburgh, Scotland, and currently lives in Europe. She writes fiction and poetry and has had work published in online and printed magazines, books and literary annuals. Kristy has had two stories appear in previous *Ghastlings:* 'The Conjurer' in Book Five and 'The Hill' in Book Eight.

BESS LOVEJOY is the author of *Rest in Pieces: The Curious Fates of Famous Corpses* (Simon & Schuster), which the *Times Literary Supplement* said contained 'something to dismay everyone.' She is a former editor on the *Schott's Almanac* series, as well as on the *Mental Floss* and *Smithsonian Magazine* websites. Her writing has appeared in *The New York Times, Lapham's Quarterly, The Boston Globe, The Public Domain Review, Atlas Obscura* and elsewhere. She has work forthcoming in *The Happy Reader* magazine as well as the Wildsam guide to Seattle, USA, where she lives. She is also a founding member of The Order of the Good Death, a US-based organisation that encourages conversations around mortality.

DAMIEN B. RAPHAEL lives and works in Oxfordshire, England. His fascination with the supernatural probably stems back to Halloween 1992, when he was scared witless by *Ghostwatch* on the BBC. Damien has had two stories appear in previous *Ghastlings*: 'The Sculpture' in Book Eight and 'Rupert's Little Brother' in Book Nine.

ALEX STEVENS is a mixed media artist who lives in Cardiff, Wales, with a cat. Primarily interested in folklore, zoology and anatomy, he tends towards the eerie and the uncanny. He recently collaborated with poet Matthew Haigh on two Sidekick Books anthologies, *Battalion* and *No, Robot, No!*, and designed book cover imagery for Salt. He can be found lurking on Twitter *@AbjectObjects*, and Instagram *@Abject_Objects*.

REBECCA PARFITT has worked in publishing for over a decade. Her debut poetry collection, *The Days After*, was published by Listen Softly London in 2017. She is currently working on a book of macabre short stories for which she won a Writers' Bursary from Literature Wales in 2020. Two stories from this collection have been published in the *New Gothic Review*, 2020. Her first film, 'Feeding Grief to Animals' was recently commissioned by the BBC & FfilmCymruWales. She lives in the Llynfi Valley, Wales, with her partner and daughter. *rebeccaparfitt.com*

RHYS OWAIN WILLIAMS is a writer and editor from Swansea, Wales. His first poetry collection, *That Lone Ship*, was published by Parthian in 2018. Rhys also runs *The Crunch* – a multimedia poetry magazine (*crunchpoetry.com*). In addition to all things ghastly, Rhys is interested in folklore, urban myth and psychogeography. He lives in a terraced house near the sea with his partner and a black cat named Poe. *rhysowainwilliams.com*

NATHANIEL WINTER-HEBERT is the creative director at Winter-Hébert – a studio cabin tucked into the wilds of Québec. He presides his wizardly duties as art director of *The Ghastling*, the folk-horror magazine *Hellebore*, and a myriad of countless projects that spiral off into a mandelbrot of infinity. He spends his day concocting all manners of visual curiosities, and at night conducts type experiments in his lab. *winterhebert.com*

Lightning Source UK Ltd.
Milton Keynes UK
UKHW022119171220
375284UK00003BA/13